Alice Marchak

Around Our Dinner Table

To Marion
With my best wishes -
Enjoy!
Alice Marchak

Merry Christmas
Love,
Tracy
2016

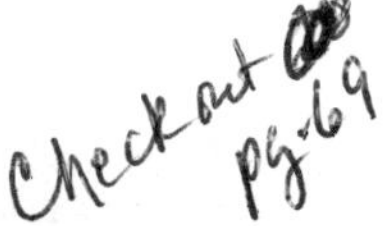

The contents of this work, including, but not limited to, the accuracy of events, people, and places depicted; opinions expressed; permission to use previously published materials included; and any advice given or actions advocated are solely the responsibility of the author, who assumes all liability for said work and indemnifies the publisher against any claims stemming from publication of the work.

Cover Design: Carol Julien

All Rights Reserved
Copyright © 2016 by Alice Marchak

No part of this book may be reproduced or transmitted, downloaded, distributed, reverse engineered, or stored in or introduced into any information storage and retrieval system, in any form or by any means, including photocopying and recording, whether electronic or mechanical, now known or hereinafter invented without permission in writing from the publisher.

Dorrance Publishing Co
585 Alpha Drive
Suite 103
Pittsburgh, PA 15238
Visit our website at *www.dorrancebookstore.com*

ISBN: 978-1-4809-2475-8
eISBN: 978-1-4809-2245-7

Alice Marchak

Around Our Dinner Table

Everybody has a story…and they can't wait to tell it.

My gratitude to
Susan and Tom Neas
without whose friendship and expertise
my books, especially this one, would
still be languishing in my computer
awaiting a journey to a home.

For family and friends whose names will live on as long as these words exist and are read.

Newport Beach 2015

After I wrote the two books, *Me and Marlon*, and *More Me And Marlon*, and then *Christmas a Child Is Born*, my friends and readers asked me to write more. Especially about Marlon, but I didn't want to keep writing about Brando. And, seriously, I didn't plan to write again. However, in emails with a friend, Beverly Wilk, we discussed writing short stories, and she challenged me to write a one sentence short story which produced "Cloudburst" and a flurry of emails.

Cloudburst

Pitter and patter, two little raindrops were frolicking with raindrop friends on their thundercloud home in the heavens when suddenly there was an unexpected cloudburst and they all were abruptly tossed out, falling rapidly to Earth amid thunder and lightning bolts, and then settled on parched desert sands where they were immediately swallowed up and were no more.

Beverly critiqued. "Sad and much too long."

So, I rewrote...

Pitter and patter, two little raindrops were frolicking on their thundercloud home when suddenly there was a cloudburst and they were abruptly tossed out, falling on parched desert sands, swallowed up, and were no more.

"Too long" came back from Bev.

I tried again...

Pitter and patter were playing on a thundercloud when suddenly there was a cloudburst and they were tossed out, falling on parched deserts sands, and disappeared.

"Still too long" she answered.

Then I wrote...

Pitter and patter, two raindrops fell to Earth where they were washed into a storm drain that emptied into the Pacific, and were lost at sea.

"What happened to the desert?" Bev replied.

I decided to ignore her.

Let her wonder.

After this, if anyone asked when I was going to write another book, I would reply: "I'm writing short stories." I wasn't, of course, but since I had *Cloudburst* to showcase I pulled it off for a very long time. It was wonderful fun.

Soon I began to seriously think about it, which produced another short story, *Clean Out the Refrigerator Casserole*, then another, *Memories of Spring and the Crack of the Bat*, and another, *Opportunities Lost*, along with *Thanksgiving*, and *Wishes*. But these languished in my computer.

So, when asked about my short stories, I would say I had a few stories written, but had writer's block. That took me through another year.

By this time, I really didn't think I would write a book of short stories. Nevertheless, after another night of storytelling around our dining table, I felt inspired and began to write again. Thus this book.

So – the stories are inspired by true events.

Therefore, you might say this work is non-fiction and fiction. The source of the stories were gathered from those told around our dining table with family and friends at dinner. The lunch-bunch added a few more. Some of the stories are short. Some are long, and some longer still. But I did start out with the intention of writing a book of "Short Short Stories" to satisfy Bev, if no one else.

In that, I didn't succeed.

In using names of my family, they, as well as friends, were all kind enough to allow me to use their names, for which I'm grateful. They were contributors at the dining table along with a few friends whose very short stories I picked up at lunch and will be recognized by their acquaintances.

~ Alice Marchak

Contents

Around Our Dinner Table

As we often did, we discussed events in our lives when we (family and friends) all sat around the dinner table having a home-cooked dinner with delicious homemade breads, pies, cakes, or puddings. There was always something about the aroma of food cooking, roasting, or baking that mellowed everyone and brought memories and comparisons of other like dinners. Then branching into people we ate with and places in which we ate. No one left the table as one story ran into another and hot tea, coffee, or wine was constantly being replenished. More times than not, the lively talk took us around the world, as most owned businesses or were employed in jobs that included extensive travelling.

The discussion usually started with: "Remember when..." and we were off. Each tried to top the other with something that had happened in his or her life. This particular evening it started out with stories of food and restaurants, and it didn't take long to get to the subject of restaurants and dates. I confess, if we were handing out prizes, I would have won first prize hands down that night with my unexpected revelation of a first date.

I had met this man-about-town who asked me to dinner. First, let me say I was twenty-two at the time, and I was not dating boys my own age – I was dating "older" men in their late twenties, early thirties, or forties. The reason: they were men who were working on their own – usually lawyers, architects, writers, businessmen – not someone living at home, working now and again, going to college, or trying to make it in the movies. I had gone through that phase.

This particular man was older, had his own thriving business, and had it made. I felt comfortable knowing I wouldn't need to worry when I ordered dinner if he had enough money to cover the check.

First Date

It was our first date. I wore a new dress for the first time too. It was white, which showed off my tan. It draped in Grecian style, which fell below my knee, as was the current length at that time. It was made out of a new age material that the tag, when I purchased it, stated in bold black letters DO NOT DRY CLEAN. WASH ONLY. With this, I wore three-inch high heels and gold jewelry – an upper arm spiral bracelet with a large dangling rough cut amethyst stone. It was summertime, and since it was California, I needed no wrap.

He complimented me when he saw me, saying, "How lovely you look – I like your dress."

Money well spent on that dress, I thought.

He had the reputation of being a big spender, so I wasn't surprised when he took me to an upscale, posh steakhouse – you know, dim lights, candlelight, and a long stem red rose in a vase on the pristine white tablecloth with a napkin folded in place, plus a sparkling glass and gleaming silver. The waiters were in black trousers with tuxedo satin stripe, white shirts, and black tie. They were so erect – walk tall, chin up, nose in the air formal.

Our table was not ready. Apologies were accepted and we were escorted to a booth in the bar with drinks of our choice; "compliments of the house." It was quite obvious by the greeting and treatment my date frequented the place.

I don't like liquor, so I wasn't much of a drinker. He was having a martini, which was the cocktail drink of the day at that time, so I said I'd have one too. It was a very dry gin martini with two olives. After a few sips on an empty stomach, I hadn't eaten anything since noon, I could feel the effects of the gin. I knew better, but stupidly kept sipping as we exchanged flirtatious small talk.

After two martinis, we were told our table was ready. When I rose to follow the waiter, I knew I had been drinking – two too much. I didn't realize it at the time, but they were double martinis. I made it to the table without incident and immediately dove into the bread and butter as soon as the waiter set a dinner roll on my dish. My date, observing this, naturally assumed I was hungry, for he immediately ordered for us and asked the waiter to hurry the food while I continued to eat the bread and butter, hoping to sober up.

In a very short time, the food arrived. We were served this enormous Porterhouse steak, at least an inch thick, and the biggest baked potato I ever saw on a large oval platter, not the usual round dinner plate. A vegetable was on a side dish. There was ketchup and the House steak sauce encased in silver on the table.

He extended the ketchup to me, which I took. Now, even in my intoxicated state, I remembered my table manners and knew enough not to give the bottom of the ketchup bottle a whack or two to get it flowing. Since I wasn't going to whack its bottom, I turned it straight up and out gurgled one half bottle of ketchup in a rapid stream.

"Oops," I said, then with a broad smile I handed him the bottle across the table, which he exchanged for the steak sauce, and also exchanged the smile as he accepted the bottle. Since the ketchup experience, I was ready for the steak sauce and tilted it halfway. Nothing came out, so I gave it what I thought was a little jerky shake, and it spurted out, skidding across the top of the ketchup, settling in a wide gooey brown and red streak on the pristine white tablecloth and was being absorbed. The hovering waiter immediately rushed over and made a big deal out of something I was prepared to ignore. He produced a napkin and, lifting the silver, covered the offending blob and apologized for the steak sauce spurting out – as if it was the bottle's fault and not mine.

My date, I thought, seemed to take it all in stride for he murmured, "Bon appétit," and cut into his steak. Tasting the morsel he again murmured, "Hm-m-m perfect."

What a nice man, I thought. Then, knife and fork in hand, I smiled at him and returned "Bon appétit" while I started cutting into my steak. I pushed the knife forward then back as I smiled across the table at him, and before I knew it, when I pulled the knife back, the juice from the steak, plus the half bottle of ketchup and another of steak sauce, caused the humungous Porterhouse steak to skid off my platter, hit me in the breastbone, and slide down my white dress, disappearing into my lap.

My date's eyes and mouth flew open. Shocked speechless, he just stared. And I, I reached down, gingerly picked up the dripping huge steak from my lap, and plopped it on the platter. I rose, covered with this blood red ketchup and steak sauce mess from chest to knees, and with great aplomb, said, "Excuse me, I'm going to the ladies room," turned and walked by the hovering waiter who stood frozen in a state of shock.

I dripped ketchup and sauce as I made my way to the ladies room with as much dignity as a tipsy girl could muster. Surprisingly, there was no ladies' maid in the powder room in this high class restaurant. I had to fend for myself. I recalled the tag on the dress which stated: DO NOT DRY CLEAN – WASH ONLY. And I thought, "What luck!" You must remember, I was drunk. Who else would think they were lucky?

I took paper towels, wet them, and tried to remove the mess. The paper towels disintegrated and didn't help. So, I filled the sink with hot water, squirted the liquid soap into my hand, and transferred it to the basin. Then I took off my dress and put it into the sink. This dress, with all its draping, didn't require a bra, so I didn't wear one – I just had on nude colored Dior satin panties trimmed in wide lace, which blended in with my summer tan – consequently, I looked nude.

There I stood next to one of the two basins in my high heels, panties, and upper arm bracelet, sloshing my dress up and down in the soapy water. I was in the down motion when the door opened and an elderly, white-haired lady walked in, looked at me bent over the sink, and screamed. I turned to her, semi-nude, hands dripping with soap suds and the dress, to explain.

She screamed, "Get away from me! Get away!" She turned to go back out, then remembered why she came into the ladies room and ran into the toilet stall, slammed and locked the door.

While she was in there, I stood at her closed door, soap suds dripping off my raised elbows, and tried to explain what had happened when another girl came in, took a look at me, and didn't know quite how to react to this naked, tipsy lady standing there in high heels, so she turned her back and stood uncertain. I returned to the sink and sloshed some more while I tried to tell her what had happened. Ignoring me, she hurried into a stall and locked the door while I continued sloshing.

I was able to get all of the ketchup and steak sauce out of the dress. Rinsed it, wrung it out, and then wrapped the dress in paper towels, which I hoped would get most of the moisture out. By this time, I was aware it would not get dry.

In the meantime, the first woman, not looking at me, got out of there as fast as she could and so did the second girl.

Next came a rapping at the door. Hiding behind the door, I cracked it open. The waiter wanted to know if everything was all right – my date had sent him to find me.

I said I was drying my dress and I should be out soon. "Give him another drink," I suggested and swiftly closed door.

I squeezed as much water as I was going to get out of the dress, so I put the damp dress on. The waist was now under my bust (small bust) and it was thigh high, and instead of loose and flowing it was skin tight. It had shrunk! Today I would have been in style, but not then.

I had no recourse but to take the dress off. I again filled the basin with hot water, immersed the dress, squeezed out most of the water, then took the dress and proceeded to stretch it when the door opened and another girl entered and froze in place, startled.

Arms wide, I explained, "My dress shrunk and I'm trying to stretch it."

Wide-eyed, she just looked at me, then proceeded to lock herself in the toilet stall. I decided I wouldn't tell her about the steak. I thought, let her think there was some "nut" in the ladies room doing her laundry. At this point, I was beyond caring. She too got out of there fast without a word of curiosity or sympathy as I wiggled into the dress. I had stretched the dress to knee length, but instead of flowing, now it was formfitting.

I went back to the table in the damp dress – the table had been cleared in my absence. My date had finished eating. He stood, silently staring at me. Gathering up my purse from the table, I solemnly said, "May we leave?" And before he could say anything, I turned and headed towards the door. He followed.

While we waited for the car to be brought around, it occurred to me he had already settled the bill as he didn't suggest we stay so I could have dinner. He just commiserated with me, took me home, saw me to the door, and made a swift getaway. I prayed he was gentleman enough not to mention my name when he entertained his friends about his date.

He was never heard from again.

Around Our Dinner Table

When Thanksgiving nears I usually send greetings to several friends. And, much to my surprise, I received an amusing reply from one, Bernard, also wishing me a "Happy Turkey Day" with the hope I didn't "have to kill a bird too" as his neighbor did every year. Bernard went on to explain that each year she raised a turkey, and when November rolled around she killed it for Thanksgiving dinner, but only "after getting it soused on several shots of whiskey."

This brought a chuckle and remembrance of Thanksgiving past when I was a child of about ten.

I wrote about it and made copies. Jumping in when I thought there was a lull in the conversation at our Thanksgiving Day dinner, I gave it to our guests, numbering twenty-two, to read.

Thanksgiving Turkey

My father went to a turkey shoot each year held for charity. All I knew about the turkey shoot was it raised a great deal of money to feed the poor on Thanksgiving Day. They didn't shoot turkeys, but a target, and the best shot won a huge tom turkey. Since this was Pennsylvania in the shadow of the Poconos where there are some great hunters, there were a number of excellent marksmen who each year vied for the turkey. We didn't have any shotguns – my mother wouldn't allow any guns around with children in the house. But my father was a good shot, so I heard. He probably learned how to shoot before he married and had children.

Being a bootlegger during prohibition, I knew he had a gun because periodically I would feel around the front seat of his Buick touring car to see if there was any money that had fallen out of his and other men's pockets and had lodged between the leather seat cushion. On one occasion, my little hand felt something. The something was a gun. So, I imagine when he and his friends said they were going to target practice, that's probably what he used. At any rate, we can assume he was a good shot because that year he won the prize – the huge, huge to a ten-year-old eyes, beautiful live tom turkey.

We first knew he had won when we saw him getting out of his Buick touring car with this beautiful big turkey that led my proud father up the back garden walk by what seemed to be a long rope-like harness leash.

My sisters, brother, and I were playing tag in the garden with neighboring children. We all stopped running, and then screamed. Naturally, we were all excited; we had never seen a live turkey, and certainly not one in our garden.

My mother rushed out of the house to find out what the sudden squealing from us children was all about. I recall she stood at the porch railing momentarily frozen in amazement while she took in the scene. She let a few minutes go by, then my mother called out to my father with grave concern, asking him what we were going to do with "that turkey."

My father loudly called out, "Eat it!" to which she replied in a louder voice:

"And who's going to kill it?"

The question just hung in the air, for that silenced my father as there was no reply to her query.

It didn't take long for a lively discussion about what was to be done with the turkey to take place. My father couldn't just stand around with squealing children running about and an equally excited turkey straining on a leash with my mother angrily proclaiming he never should have brought a live turkey home. He, raising his voice over us, contended he won it and wanted the children to see it. If he was proud of his achievement when he arrived with his prize, she was certainly deflating his ego in a hurry.

The turkey war had started, and progressed from there.

We were all frightened by the turkey as it would run hither and yon. So, the heated conversation between my parents was drowned out by screams. But the upshot of the commotion was my father, over my mother's objections, put his prize turkey in the cellar, which I must say now my mother was right; it was the wrong place for a huge tom turkey.

Our basement had shelves along one wall where all the glass mason jars my mother "put up" each fall stood row upon row. We had a bushel of apples on a table. We had a large family, at this time, eight children and two adults, so we always had a half-bushel or pecks of fruit on that table, plus a stalk of bananas hanging in the stairwell.

If putting the turkey in the cellar was a mistake, then taking the leash off instead of tying it off on a post was the second. The turkey had free rein of the cellar, and every time someone wanted something from the cellar, they ran off screaming from a screeching, mad turkey. It must be remembered our boiler was also in the basement, and it had to be attended by my father, so he too was not exempt from attacks. Daily, there were reports of destruction in the cellar, which, of course, was saved up to greet my father when he arrived home. As soon as he opened the door, he got a double whammy, for one of us would tell him gravely what happened in the cellar, with another child putting their two cents in.

Then my mother would loudly cap it all off with: "You've got to get rid of that turkey!"

He'd pour himself a stiff drink, or two.

The turkey war continued on every day and night. Whenever my father came into my mother's sight, she reminded my father of his mistakes, starting with winning the turkey and not donating it to the Salvation Army for the poor, to bringing it home, to scaring the children, to not putting it in the three-car garage as she had suggested and which he refused to do because he didn't want his cars pooped on and scratched, to reminding him of the time he decided we ought to learn how to ride and he bought a horse instead of a pony. He brought it home, and we were all too terrified of the stomping, snorting huge animal to get on its back, let alone near it. Everything he ever did wrong was dredged up and thrown at him.

The turkey fiasco raged on until a few days before Thanksgiving when my father made his biggest mistake. He asked my mother to kill the turkey, saying my twelve and fourteen-year-old brothers could hold the turkey while she chopped off its head!

It's a good thing the axe he wanted her to do it with was in the cellar with the doomed turkey, or you know whose head would be on the block.

After all he went through, what was he thinking?

Need I say more?

A few days later, my father corralled several neighbors to what could only be called a roundup. Amid much yelling, running about the large basement chasing the screeching, attacking turkey, when next I saw my father; he was no longer a proud man as he carried the beautiful trussed tom turkey, whose neck had been spared, across the garden lawn to the open back door of his Buick touring car.

We never knew what happened to the turkey. Nobody dared ask nor dared mention turkey for a very long time in our house without getting "the look" from my mother. "The look" stopped us cold when forgetting turkey was taboo.

We had goose for Thanksgiving that year and turkey wasn't mentioned, nor did it appear on our Thanksgiving dinner table until we were all grown many, many years later.

The Look

Lauren Bacall of movie fame was known as "The Look." If you're expecting to read about Bacall, you'll be disappointed, for "The Look" I'm referring to is the one mothers of my generation used to control their children. My mother had "The Look" down to perfection.

Especially when out in public, you had to mind your manners and behave or you got "The Look" which meant, "Stop what you're doing! Behave yourself! Wait until you get home; you're going to hear about this!" It all depended on what you were doing to cause "The Look," but whatever it was, "The Look" put an immediate halt to it.

When you see mothers and misbehaving children in public today, it makes one wonder what happened to "The Look." When did it fall by the wayside? Why didn't I notice it had disappeared before this?

Isn't it too bad "The Look" hadn't been passed down from generation to generation?

Around Our Dinner Table

My childhood remembrance led to many, many Thanksgiving stories, as everyone around the dinner table always tried to top one another. When I could get a word in, I was wont to tell of a few throughout the years spent with Marlon Brando, who I worked for, and Thanksgiving at his home.

Each year when Thanksgiving rolled around, Marlon too would recall what happened at Thanksgiving dinners and we'd have a merry old time remembering.

I had written about a Thanksgiving with Marlon in my book, *Me and Marlon*. I titled it "Aunts Don't Go to Marlon's Picnics." I'd like to share it again.

Aunts Don't Go to Marlon's Picnics

It was early the day after Thanksgiving. Marlon's Aunt Bette called and asked me to please, please take her off Marlon's Thanksgiving Day guest list. That was my first clue Thanksgiving dinner at Marlon's was a fiasco again. This was now three years in a row!

What was it about Thanksgiving? What was it about Marlon and dinner parties?

Marlon's sister, Jocelyn, each year made the turkey dressing their mother had made for them when they were growing up. It was a favorite of Marlon's, and he would look forward to it each year. Jocelyn would arrive at Marlon's house Thanksgiving morning and put the stuffed turkey in the oven, and then return to her home in Rustic Canyon.

This particular year, Marlon told Jocelyn, "Sleep in, I'll put the turkey in the oven in the morning."

Before I left for my home at the beach, I typed out all the instructions in regard to the turkey, as per Jocelyn's request, and taped them where Marlon wouldn't miss them – on the refrigerator.

As Bette told me, the family all arrived, had drinks, and some lively conversation. When they asked, "Isn't it time to eat?" they discovered the turkey was still in the refrigerator.

Marlon's solution was for Jocelyn to put the turkey in the oven; they could have another drink, set the table, get the rest of the food prepared, and by that time the turkey would be done and ready to eat.

Marlon did not know it took hours to roast a stuffed turkey, and he put the blame on me when next we spoke. Marlon was dyslexic and couldn't see very well. He reminded me that knowing this, I had written down the instructions.

He saw the paper taped on the refrigerator door and couldn't read it, so ignored it, never thinking it had anything to do with the turkey.

Usually, if I left Marlon notes I told him I was leaving a note and what was in it, and seeing the note, it would remind him what I had told him. But he wasn't around when I left and I didn't call him from the beach to tell him the note was instructions for roasting the turkey, there was a magnifying glass on my desk, and to call me if there was a problem.

Explaining this to Bette did no good – she had enough. "Marlon boiled hot dogs!" Bette fumed. "Never again will I accept an invitation for Thanksgiving at his house. I thought last year was bad enough, but this was too much!"

The last year Bette referred to, Toto the St. Bernard, had stolen the turkey from the kitchen. When I saw the dog lope by the living room window with the turkey, I got up and left the room motioning to Marlon. He got my drift, followed me outside, and I told him what I had seen. Then we chased Toto around the garden, cornering him outside Marlon's bathroom where Marlon wrested the turkey out of his jaws. But Toto got away with the drumstick and thigh he had clenched between his teeth. Carrying the mutilated turkey, Marlon and I then stole around the house into the kitchen where, amid laughter, Marlon tried to hide the gaping hole with a bunch of parsley. It didn't work. It still looked like a turkey with a missing leg and thigh.

Marlon had persuaded me to have Thanksgiving with him and the rest of his family, and now Marlon was asking, "Aren't you glad you stayed?" as we looked at each other laughing, trying to decide what to do.

The cook was lying down in my office, still in shock, having had a panic attack over the disappearance of the turkey. She had taken it out of the oven and placed it on a platter on the counter, then went to the bathroom only to find the huge turkey missing from the platter when she returned.

We decided it was best to slice the remaining turkey instead of presenting it at the table.

I took over the kitchen and urged Marlon back to the family, telling him, "Don't say anything about the dog and the turkey." But Marlon thought otherwise, it was too good not to tell. Of course, everyone was hysterical with laughter as Marlon dramatized us chasing Toto around the garden and having caught him, his wrestling match with the dog to retrieve our Thanksgiving dinner. Bette was not amused by the drama and, when dinner was served, she refused to eat the turkey retrieved from the dog.

Now Thanksgiving this year, the turkey was uncooked in the refrigerator, and there were "hot dogs".

That did it. Enough was enough for her.

Though she was very fond of Marlon, Bette meant what she said; she never accepted an invitation to Thanksgiving dinner at Marlon's home again.

Around Our Dinner Table

You're probably unaware I live in Newport Beach, California, as well as the rest of my family. It has two huge, beautiful shopping centers, well one, Fashion Island, and is in Newport Beach, and the other, South Coast Plaza is only several miles away in Costa Mesa.

Our teens can usually be found at either. "I'm going to the mall," is heard as they hurry out the door on their cell phones, although they could be alluding to either nearby Westminster or Irvine malls too.

But, we also have mini malls where Ross, TJMax, Marshalls, Pier 1, etc. and some very good restaurants can be found, and these are usually where we "older folks" can be found too because they're in our neighborhoods, closer parking, one stop shopping. Also, the price is right! Who doesn't like a bargain?

Since they are surrounded by restaurants, when dining, someone is sure to say at the end of the meal, "Let's pop over to TJ Max and walk this off." The store depends upon where we're dining. But, I can't pretend we only "pop over" to walk off the dessert after dining at one of the many, many fine restaurants on 17th Street in our neighborhood.

The Kitchen Rug

Ever since the Ross store came to town, it's like a magnet. We're drawn to it whenever we have a few hours to spend in finding the best bargain or bargains.

When sitting around with nothing to do, it's, "Let's go over to Ross's." So, it was not unusual for me to see my sisters, Marty and Peggy, roaming the aisles.

"Hi!" I greeted them, "Find anything interesting?"

"Only a fall-colored braided rug," Marty said, lifting a corner of the rag rug in Peggy's cart.

Peggy added, "We're going to try it in my kitchen. It should be a nice change from summer to fall."

After a few "see ya's" and "let me know how it turns out," we parted and continued roaming the aisles.

Our family consisted of six girls with our own apartments, or homes. So, through the years, when anyone moved or redecorated, the cry was: "Don't give anything away until I look at it!" or "I need a lamp," or whatever, "Do you have one in storage?" So, no matter whose house you went into, you invariably found something that had belonged to you or one of the others.

It was fortunate the girls married into the Marines and Air Force, and had football player friends. They were always available when called upon to get something out of storage, or transported from one house to another. When a niece married a man with a truck, it was heaven sent, for then things could be hauled from the Rancho Mirage houses in the desert to the beach houses. But this is not about all the furniture passed from house to house to house for years, this is about "the rug" purchased at Ross's one Saturday afternoon the end of August when Marty and Peggy went on a bargain hunt.

We were all at the combined birthday party for nieces, Camielle, Meghan, and Marisha when next I saw Marty and Peggy.

"How did the rug go in your kitchen?" I asked Peggy.

Rolling her eyes to the ceiling, she replied, "Go ask Marty. She'll tell you."

What was with the eye rolling? Why couldn't Peg tell me? I wondered as I looked around the den and found Marty sitting on a corner window seat where I joined her.

"Peggy said to ask you about the rug. Is she keeping it, or what?"

Marty rolled her eyes to the ceiling too, and laughed. "It's rather complicated."

"I can handle complicated. So give," I urged.

I reached for the pitcher on the table and poured some orange juice into a glass and placed it in front of Marty. If this was a long story, I figured Marty might need it.

I took a seat and Marty told me what had happened since I saw them with the rug at the Ross store. Peggy bought the rug, and she and Marty took it home to try in her kitchen. It was five by eight, and it fit nicely, but she has an all cream kitchen, and though Marty liked it, Peggy thought the fall colors in the braided rag rug – brown, gold, maroon, and green – the color of turning leaves – were too strong. Marty tried to convince her once fall set in and the rug was down a while, she'd like it. Peggy wasn't quite certain she wanted to keep it. It was a "maybe."

"I really like the rug," Marty said. "Since my kitchen is mahogany wood, I told Peggy I'll take it and see how it looks on my floor. Then if she didn't want to keep it, I'll buy it."

So, Marty rolled up the rug, and she and Peggy carried it out and again struggled putting it into Marty's car, which I must say, had hauled more than that rug. Fortunately, when Marty arrived at her house in The Bluffs, the gardeners were working across the street, and she had the heavy braided rag rug carried upstairs and rolled out on the kitchen floor by them.

"You'll have to see it!" Marty exclaimed. "It fit perfectly." The fall colors, gold, green, and brown – they all worked with my dark wood. I love it!"

"Did Peggy let you buy the rug from her?" I inquired.

Marty replied she knew Peggy was undecided, so she phoned Peggy and told her it looked so well on her kitchen floor, she'd like to keep it.

Since Peggy bought it and it was a "maybe," and Marty loved it and would like to keep it, they had to think it over and decide what to do.

Marty thought about it and figured out a solution in regard to the rug that would suit both her and hopefully Peggy. She phoned and informed her she had a solution and told Peggy to "Get a pencil and paper."

"Right," Peggy said. "Got pencil and paper."

"Now write this down and we'll both sign it." Marty then proceeded to tell Peggy her solution:

> AGREEMENT RUG
> We would both own the rug – each pay half.
> January, February, March – Peggy has rug (Marty in Rancho Mirage in the desert).
> April, May – rug in storage.
> (Rabbit rug out of storage for Easter season).
> June – rug out of storage – Peggy has rug.
> July, August, September – Marty has rug (Marty returns from desert).
> October, November – Peggy has rug.
> December – rug in storage.
> (Christmas rug out of storage for Christmas season)

Only Marty could figure complicated and make it sound like sense if they were going to divide the rug I thought, until Marty continued.

"First, there were some questions that had to be resolved."

"What about soiling the rug? What about spills? What side of the rug was Marty's and what side Peggy's?"

After much thought, Marty said she came to a decision. She phoned Peggy again and included in the "Rug Agreement":

> "Marty will have one side of the rug.
> Peggy will have the other side.
> A large baby blanket pin should be put
> on the underside to indicate Peggy's side
> when she doesn't have the rug.
> The pin put on Marty's side when it is turned over.
> Both will agree it can't be turned over
> if they spill something on their side
> and there is a stain."

Marty finished, and by this time, I understood why Peggy rolled her eyes heavenward at the mention of the rug. I couldn't refrain from asking, "Just how much did this braided kitchen rag rug cost?"

"$14.99," Marty very seriously revealed.

"You're both going to need good lawyers," I said, rolling my eyes to the heavens too, as I got up and walked away.

Around Our Dinner Table

Though not all the girls in our family had children, the nieces, nephews, grandnieces, and nephews were always greeted joyously at birth and claimed as our own.

So, now that the grandnieces and nephews are of marriage age and are married, we are all anticipating, even if they aren't. Boy, was I taken in by grandnephew Christopher when he told me he had a "surprise."

Eavesdropping Madness

"You're not going to name it Stella!"

"If it's a girl, we are! I've always wanted..."

She cut him off, shouting, "NEVER!"

Jana and Christopher had arrived for a birthday party and I could hear their conversation as they crossed the terrace and passed the open window. They had been married three years, but even before they wed, they informed the family not to expect any children until Christopher finished architectural college and she got her master's degree. Now they were arguing over names! How exciting! Maybe they would announce the news of the arrival of a little one since they were discussing names. Perhaps it would be on this visit.

I couldn't wait for them to make the announcement. I had a few names to throw in the mix and one of them was not Stella. Not that I had anything against the name. I had an Aunt Stella who I liked very much, but I didn't think Stella was a fit with Jana and Christopher.

We all, the family of eleven that is, gathered for another birthday celebration. With a family that large, twelve months in the year, and all the holidays, plus big ones like Easter, Fourth of July, Halloween, Thanksgiving, and Christmas we had every month covered – and always in departing, planning for the next get-together.

This was Meggie's birthday we were celebrating. I waited with great anticipation until the birthday girl had blown out the candles, unwrapped her gifts, and kissed and thanked everyone for Jana and Christopher to make their big announcement.

I waited in vain.

Instead, Christopher and Jana said their goodbyes; they had to get on the road to San Diego where they now lived, nearer to Christopher's architectural college. So they left – and no announcement! What a letdown!

Well, if they didn't want to announce it, what the heck, I was bursting with the news, and I couldn't keep it any longer. I clapped my hands for silence.

"I have something to tell you!"

There were shouts of, "QUIET! QUI-EEET EVERYONE!"

Someone said, "If you had an announcement, why didn't you make it before Jana and Christopher left?"

There was a silence. "Because it concerns them." I proceeded to tell what I had heard them arguing about as they arrived at my door.

A baby! This was a bombshell! Everyone was thrilled. All talked at once. No one expected this.

Everyone agreed with Jana. Stella was not going to be the name if all of us had any say in the matter. I had to get them all to swear they would keep what I had heard a secret. "And never, ever, say the name Stella."

I may have received their promise to keep the impending arrival of a little girl a secret, but I couldn't stop them talking to each other about it. The phones were kept busy with calls wondering how many months she was pregnant, the many calls asking if anyone noticed if she was showing yet, or if anyone took note of how much she had eaten at the party – was she eating for two? Baby talk went on for days.

Then Christopher sent me an email – they would like to come up to Newport Beach for the weekend and stay with me, and added they had a surprise.

Wow! The surprise! I emailed to come along; looked forward to their visit.

Immediately, it was to the phone. The news was passed around with the admonition – act surprised. For the rest of the week, it was one of great anticipation. We concluded they didn't make the announcement the week before because they didn't want to take anything away from the birthday girl's happy 21st birthday, so decided their birth announcement could be postponed. The next few days felt like years.

The weekend finally arrived and I received a text they were on the road and should be arriving in about twenty minutes. I alerted everyone at Mims and Todd's house, the overjoyed grandparents-to-be, where everyone had gathered to have a brunch celebration of the announcement.

I had a bottle of champagne cooling, hidden in the garage refrigerator. This would call for a toast, even if Jana wouldn't have a drink since she was pregnant; perhaps a sip. Christopher and I certainly would if they told me before we went to the awaiting brunch.

I heard the car pull into the driveway. Even though the door was wide open, I didn't go out to greet them. I stayed where I was, watching the ballgame on television. I didn't want to appear too anxious to hear their surprise announcement.

I rose when they entered. Christopher came in first and greeted me with a kiss. Behind was Jana with a cheery, "Hi!" I stared at her coming towards me as she was cradling a furry bundle with huge dark brown eyes and long brown ears....and she, too, kissed me hello saying, "Meet Marlon! The new addition to our family!"

"This is the surprise?" I sputtered. "A dog?"

"Yes, we got it yesterday. Isn't he just adorable?" Jana gushed. "He's an eight-week-old Cavalier King Charles Spaniel," she added.

I came out of my trance and laughed myself silly. Jana and Christopher looked at one another, and then back at me laughing my fool head off. I tried to tell them what I was laughing about, but couldn't stop laughing long enough to do so.

Finally, I wound down and confessed what I had heard and about spreading the news they were anticipating. Now it was their turn to start laughing at all of us being "baby crazy."

I held the cuddly puppy and asked, "Why Marlon?"

"I had seen Marlon Brando in *Streetcar Named Desire*, and said if I ever got a dog, I would name it Stella," Christopher confessed. "I always wanted to yell, 'Stell-aah,' like Brando, and if I had a dog, I could. But it's male. So, Jana and I decided to name him Marlon since I couldn't name him Stella."

Christopher then looked at his dog and, like Brando, yelled, "STELL-AAH!"

The pup responded with a soft "Yip, Yip," and licked my hand.

"Hey, Christopher, that's a pretty good Brando 'STELL-AAH!' I said, laughing at him.

"It should be. I've been practicing it for years," he proudly quipped, laughing while Jana just looked at both of us and shook her head.

I put Christopher and Jana's fluffy surprise back into Jana's waiting arms. "I better fortify myself and prepare to face the family," I said and produced the waiting champagne and glasses.

Christopher popped the cork and poured three glasses. We touch glasses, raised them, and yelled, "STELL-AAH!" Laughing like idiots we sipped, and then toasted loudly again. "MAAR-LON!"

The puppy softly yipped.

What a Lucky Unlucky Stroke

All his life Big Mike prided himself because he had never been to a doctor and or hospital. "Doctors couldn't cure themselves, and hospitals were where you went to die," were words he lived by.

Now in his eighty-fifth year of life, he could give you statistics about the people he knew who died in a hospital to prove it – names and numbers. Naturally, they were his own.

It was true most of his acquaintances who passed on had been rushed to a hospital, and when next he saw them they were laid out in a mortuary in a blue suit. He swore that was never going to happen to him. Why he thought this was the reason for his longevity, is anyone's guess.

Of course, Big Mike didn't take into consideration each time he had occasion to meet the young town doctor, socially or on the street, he took the time to chat, and Doc always gave of his time. These sidewalk consultations, as that is what they were, always amused Doc who was aware of Big Mike's aversion to doctors and hospitals. But Big Mike through the years held bragging rights he never had been to a doctor.

"And look at how healthy I am!" he'd boast.

Nor did he count the times after meeting Doc on the street he headed for the corner drugstore to get the over-the-counter remedy they spoke about for what was not ailing him, but someone he knew who had an ailment.

Oh, no. Never for him.

Then one night his luck ran out.

Big Mike had been a sports fan his entire life, and while watching a baseball game and loudly disagreeing with the umpire over a disputed call, he had a seizure and, fearing it was a stroke, his frantic wife, Maria, immediately called 911.

Big Mike was rushed by ambulance to the hospital where he lay surrounded by nurses and doctors – some of them attending him. He was helpless to do anything about it. Clearly he was frightened.

Hours later when Big Mike was stable and finally settled in a room, Maria and his three married children, who had also arrived, were allowed to visit. One at a time.

"Well, you finally found a way to get rid of me," Big Mike greeted his worried wife. "Put me in the hospital to die."

"Oh, shush, the doctor told me you will recover."

"Then get me out of here!"

"I see you're feeling better. I'll let the others come in; we only have a few minutes each, then I'll come back before we leave."

"Oh, ho, they've all gathered to say their last goodbye, have they?"

Sighing, Maria turned and left the room. Since speaking to the doctor, she was assured he would live to talk about his experience. Now her only concern was he would be a difficult patient while in the hospital.

"Get me out of here!" was still ringing in her ears as Maria prepared for bed. She knew she wouldn't sleep with the sound ringing in her ears, but there was nothing she could have done. Big Mike had to be hospitalized, and she knew, since he had never had a physical, the tests she had arranged with his doctor to do at the hospital now he had Big Mike in his clutches, were long overdue.

This was something she had been wanting done for years. Big Mike would have fits if he knew she and the doctor had decided to give him a complete checkup – head to toe – inside and out. He would not be out of the hospital for a few days.

The day Big Mike was confined to a bed, he was a bear. He banned his wife and children from visiting. Since they didn't want him upset, his wishes were carried out though Maria called to find out how he was behaving and progressing.

Big Mike was up and walking the halls. Soon his grumpy mood lightened. The hospital ward he was in with patients walking around gave him a different perspective. Of course, he enjoyed the pampering by the young ladies in white uniforms while they took tests prescribed by his physician.

He soon called his wife. Not yearning for her to visit, since he was determined to thwart her wishes to have him "gone." He wasn't quite over his being "mad" at her for "putting him in the hospital to die." But, in the meantime, he wanted certain personal items – his own shaving razor, comb and brush, and his robe and slippers. Added to the list was a two-pound box of chocolates.

Since when was he eating candy? A beer was more like it.

Chocolates? Maria pondered, but was happy to have the ban lifted as she was worried about Big Mike, even though she was aware he was receiving the best of care since she and her children were in daily contact with the nurse on his floor, as well as his doctor.

After her delivery, Maria discovered the chocolates were not for him but for the nurses.

"How is the food?" Maria asked.

"Better than all you were feeding me that was clogging up my arteries."

"What do you mean I clogged up your arteries?"

He ignored her. "I'm eating healthy now; more salads, more greens, and fruit. More fish."

Maria interrupted him. "Oh, you mean you're now eating the rabbit food you said I was putting on the table."

"I'm not eating it with that salad dressing you were mixing up. Now I'm eating healthy – olive oil and balsamic vinegar."

He was on a roll, but so was Maria.

"You said that too much fruit and vegetables gave you gas."

"That's because you gave me the wrong vegetables. I'm going to bring a menu home with me when I'm well enough to leave after you put me here to die. It'll list all the healthy food I'm to eat."

"And are you bringing the chef home with you?" Maria asked.

"There you go, you know if I have a healthy diet I could live to be a hundred. You wouldn't like that, would you?" He continued to bait her.

"Who cooked your meals before you came in here? Aren't you the one bragging you lived eighty-five years without a sick day in your life?"

"I don't want to talk about it." His usual retort when he was backed into a corner.

Maria was glad to see he was his feisty old self and he wasn't giving the staff a bad time in regard to the changes in his diet.

Since he had banned visitors, and knowing his feelings about their profession and hospitals, his physician and the nurses set out to change his mind with the utmost attention. Big Mike ate it up. Now he was buying them chocolates.

His family couldn't be happier with the great progress he had made. He'd be out of the hospital soon.

Each day Maria continued to visit, bringing the list of things he wanted and always some treats for the nurses.

After a few days, his doctor came by his room with good news. All the tests were finished and results were in. He was well enough to go home. He did not have a stroke.

What did the doctor know? Big Mike had a convenient relapse. His wife was called and told he was not leaving. Concerned, Maria rushed to the hospital. When she arrived at his bedside, she saw he was well and wanted to take him home.

Big Mike insisted he was not well enough to leave. What did the doctors know? He insisted on more tests and refused to leave, so Maria went home without him.

During Big Mike's stay, he had become the darling of the nurses, not only because he was Big Mike, but he was not bedridden, so he visited all the other patients, giving them words of wisdom learned in his eighty-five years. He comforted and sympathized. He walked with them up and down the hall, popped in and out of their rooms getting them another pillow or blanket, and called the nurses when someone was in trouble.

All the patients on the floor waited for his visits. It was a happy floor. Except for one patient whose room was off limits to everyone. It was a young man. Big Mike was curious about him and, of course, didn't hesitate asking the nurses about his condition. The nurses didn't give him any information. Nevertheless, Big Mike learned, by asking everyone on the floor, he may have tried to kill himself. But no one was privy as to how. He did learn, however, all sharp objects were forbidden.

Big Mike saw him walking the hall with a male nurse late in the evening and joined. It wasn't long before he had him discussing the baseball game Big Mike knew he had on earlier in the evening. The next night Big Mike joined the walk in the hall again. It didn't take long for him to discover the young man had attempted suicide.

The next morning when Big Mike was told he was being discharged, he immediately wanted to see his doctor. He wasn't feeling well, and since they didn't need his room, the doctor gave him another day. This would give him more time getting used to his new regiment the doctor had prescribed, but told him it was his last day; he was being discharged in the morning.

Again, Maria was informed Big Mike was not being released. She and everyone else knew he was faking it, but they had wanted to be certain all his tests were completed and he really was ready to leave. Though, if it continued this way, Maria would have a family meeting to determine what to do about Big Mike. Knocking him over the head and abducting him came to mind and was immediately discarded because he'd probably demand he needed hospitalization.

Big Mike took advantage of this reprieve and went to the young man's room. "Do you want company?" he asked walking into his room and shut the door before he could reply.

"You can't be in here! You must leave!" his male nurse exclaimed when he found Big Mike in the room.

"I invited him in," the young man said. "I want him to stay."

Alarmed, but not wanting trouble, the nurse left. After consultation, the doctor and nurses took this as a big improvement, Big Mike was allowed to enter his room during the day at will.

The next day Big Mike was scheduled for discharge and he called his wife and told her not to come to pick him up, but to drop off the box of goodies he had ordered for all the patients and for the nurses at the nurses' station.

Maria was beyond confused. Something had to be done. But what?

There had been a great number of emergencies during the night at the hospital, therefore a number of beds were needed. Since Big Mike was being discharged that morning, his bed was one being turned over.

Big Mike returned to his room after making his early rounds of the floor just as they were preparing to strip his bed. The nurse informed him his room was needed and he was being discharged. He jumped on the bed and refused to move.

They needed the room. He had to go. Big Mike insisted he was not released, so they wheeled the bed out into the hall where he remained all day. Another patient had been wheeled in and now occupied his room. He immediately became too sick to leave. They ignored him. They let him walk with the patients, visit their rooms, and talk to the suicidal patient. They were busy elsewhere.

In the meantime, Maria begged him to come home. She was tired running back and forth with his demands and clothes he refused. Nothing she said or did could make him leave. He slept in the hall.

During that time, Big Mike finally broke through the young man's reticence to speak about what brought him to the hospital. Also, Big Mike had learned his young wife had been coming to see him every day, but he refused to see her. Big Mike prevailed upon the young man to see his grieving wife.

"I can't see her! I look like hell! I need a shave and a haircut."

"You're right. Go shave."

Big Mike was happy he had finally convinced him to allow his wife to visit.

The young man confessed he didn't have anything to shave with or trim his hair. So, Big Mike got his scissors and straight razor and brought it in and gave him a trim. The young man was shaving with Big Mike's straight razor when his male nurse came by with his medication and pushed the panic button when he saw the patient with the razor at his throat, and noted the scissors within reach.

The floor was in an uproar.

That was the last straw.

Notwithstanding the fact the young man's wife finally visited, Big Mike was virtually thrown out of the hospital.

Big Mike had slept on his bed in the hall for a few days, but now the bed was gone, so he sat in a wheelchair he found. His possessions were in a draw-string disposable bag at the nurses' station. His wife was called once again to pick him up, but told not to bring his clothes as they planned to let him think they were taking him for a test and wheel him out in his robe and bedroom slippers to her car.

They were happy, yet sad, to put him out. They would miss him. But they were mistaken if they thought they had seen the last of Big Mike.

Big Mike made the hospital a mission.

Once a week he drove to the hospital, bringing a box of chocolates and other goodies. Lying he was a relative, Big Mike made the rounds dispensing goodies and visiting the patients in "his" ward.

To Kill or Not to Kill

To kill or not to kill, that was the problem. There is a fly in the apartment – I think there is only one, but I've seen it in the bedroom, living room, bathroom, and now in the kitchen while I'm preparing something to eat before I'm off to work at the studio, Paramount.

When I was a child and we had a fly problem, my mother retrieved the fly swatter out of hiding, and that was the end of the fly, but only when my father wasn't around. He didn't believe in killing anything, so ants roamed and flies flew when he was around. But my mother did not want flies in her kitchen or on our food. Even though we were careful when we went in and out the door not to let a fly in, sometimes the screen doors did not close rapidly enough and you'd hear one of us holler:

"A fly got into the house!" and we'd scramble for the hidden fly swatter to "get it" before my father came home and saw us.

Other times when he was around and a fly or two was in the house, my mother would give each of us a tea towel, then she'd open the screen door and we'd all swish the tea towel through the air chasing the fly or flies out the door.

You have no idea how embarrassing it was when one day a girlfriend came by and saw us all waving towels toward the open door, chasing flies. As she entered, we all screamed, "Close the screen quick!" Then, we tried to explain we were chasing two flies out. She looked at us as if we were very odd indeed, as she said, "We kill any that comes into our home."

We never took the time to explain my father and all living creatures, and now here I was all grown up, away from home, and a fly was in the apartment following me from room to room as if it owned the place.

I put my toasted scrambled egg sandwich on a plate and brought my cup of breakfast tea to the pullout breadboard from under the counter, scooted onto the kitchen stool, and opened the morning paper to see what happened in the world while I slept. This fly didn't get on my plate of food, but came and walked unafraid over the page I was reading. When I turned the page it flew off, and then returned and walked around. This went on all through breakfast while I read. I did my dishes while the fly watched from the rim of the sink, not realizing its minutes were numbered.

I didn't have a fly swatter, so I rolled up the newspaper the fly had read with me that morning and stalked the fly. It kept eluding me, but, determined, I kept swatting and swatting and swatting. After chasing the fly from room to room, swatting like a mad woman and missing, I stopped and said to myself, "This is crazy. You're going to work up a sweat chasing and swatting at this fly." So, I toss the paper down in disgust. The fly landed on the newspaper and calmly walked around as I stared in disbelief. Glaring at it, I yelled, "It wasn't a game! Didn't you know your life was on the line?"

The fly just ignored me.

"You win. I'm going to let you live," I said, giving up. I gathered my purse and keys and headed for the door, a sore loser. I opened the door and paused – I had a few more words for my nemesis. "Have a good time! I'll get you later!" *Chew on that*, I thought as I slammed the door.

Thoughts of my houseguest was the furthest thing from my mind till I returned home and was, again, followed around the apartment. I questioned whether the pest had a good day, and if it missed me. Growing up, we had always talked to our pets, but there is a difference in talking to a full-grown, very bright German shepherd who you knew understood commands, and a housefly. But it wasn't long before I changed my mind, and the fly became a pet instead of a pest, for I found myself telling it where I was going and to follow me, which it did, then sat and commanded it to do certain things and it would.

Now I know you're thinking, "This girl has gone 'round the bend." Well, you wouldn't be the only one. But that fly not only fascinated me but it amused me no end. We developed a very friendly relationship, for I no longer played the "fold up the newspaper and chase the fly game." Each morning we read the newspaper together, along with me telling it I was going to turn the page and it would fly away and return after I did so.

This may be hard to believe, but it's true. Why would I lie? I'm really not a quirky girl, but this fly sure had my number.

My sister, Mary Christmas, who was living at March Air Force Base, usually came to Hollywood to visit me for a few days when her Air Force husband was away on government business. She had arrived for the weekend and had settled in. Standing in the kitchen doorway she asked:

"Who were you talking to?" She looked at me queerly as she knew we were the only two in the apartment.

"Oh, I was telling my pet fly we had company, and you were here for a few days."

"You have a pet!"

She was surprised because I had been urged to get a pet, but I didn't want a pet in an apartment, plus I didn't want one I had to leave while I went to work or travelled. Frankly, I didn't want the responsibility.

"Yes, don't you see the fly?" I replied.

The fly walked around the top of the Coke can I had opened.

"You're kidding!" She laughed, poking me with her bony elbow.

"No, I'm not kidding. I've got it trained. It follows me all over the apartment and does what I tell it to do," I bragged.

She went to poke me again, but I moved too fast. Once was enough. She missed. She continued looking at me strangely and laughing.

So I said, "I'm going to go from room to room. Observe, the fly will follow me."

"I'll go with you."

She and I went down the hall to the bathroom. Soon the fly appeared, then we continued throughout the apartment – to the bedroom, and living room, the fly following.

I sat down on the sofa and picked up a book I had been reading. The fly flew and sat on the book. I told the fly I was going to open the book. It flew away. I opened the book. The fly came back. I turned pages twice, and each time I told the fly I would and it flew away and returned.

Then I told the fly: "I'm going to close the book, you better get on my finger." I held out my finger on my left hand and the fly flew onto it. I put the book aside and told the fly: "I'm going to bring my hand up to my face and blow – you should fly away." The fly had followed my commands. That my sister was amazed was an understatement.

"I can't believe it! I can't believe it! I saw it with my own eyes." Still, she wanted more.

"Okay, put your finger out. I'll ask it to go onto your finger, and then I'll have you blow it off."

Which she did. After the experiment, she only said in wonder, "I never knew a fly could be a pet."

That was two of us.

The following day I received a call at work from May-May. She was hysterical as only she could be. She had forgotten the fly was in the apartment, had opened the sliding glass door to the balcony, and left it open while she lounged in the sunshine. Suddenly, she saw the fly flying about. She tried chasing it back inside, but she said she thought it became frightened by her waving her hands, chasing it, and yelling, "Go back inside!" and it flew away.

I consoled her the best I could over the phone, saying flies were a dime a dozen, another would come by.

"But that was a trained fly. That was your pet. I'll leave the door open – maybe it'll come back. I'm so sorry," she wailed.

It didn't find its way back. But that wasn't the end of the fly.

A few months later, we were both visiting my mother at the beach. My sisters, Boots and Marty, and Marty's gentleman friend, Frank, and a couple others were all at dinner with us. The subject being discussed was pets and May-May piped up:

"Alice had a pet fly," then sorrowfully continued, "and I opened the sliding glass door to the balcony and it flew away and never came back."

She went on and on about how sorry she was to have opened the door and my pet fly got out and never returned.

All were silent at the table, but all eyes were on me. I knew they were wondering who was crazier, May-May or me. I pooh-poohed her outburst, but she insisted I tell them about my pet fly, and since they were now all ears, I did.

By this time, Frank, who Marty later married, looked at me as if I had escaped from the funny farm or was let out of the attic for dinner.

My sisters and the others looked at me quite worried too when, lo and behold, May-May squealed, "There's a fly! Maybe you could talk to it!"

Sure enough there was a fly walking across the dinner table. Everyone was quietly looking at the fly and looking at me. It looked similar in color to mine. We all watched it walk toward me, then I put out my finger and asked it to hop on my finger. Holding my breath, I watched it come toward my finger and fly onto it.

I told everyone, "Stay quiet," and told the fly, "I'm going to blow you off my finger and I want you to come back." It did so. Then I asked the skeptic Frank to hold out his finger and I told the fly, "I want you to fly to Frank's finger." I blew, and the fly flew off and returned to Frank's extended finger. I then asked Frank to blow, which he did, and the fly flew off.

I didn't think after that dinner Frank would marry into the family, but he took a big leap and did.

Through the years, I thought Frank had forgotten about the fly episode, I knew I did. But one election evening at Marty and Frank's Balboa Bay Club apartment when everyone had been raising a few too many glasses in celebration, a "happy" guest cornered me and with liquid courage was amorously expressing his affection while I was fending him off with my hand every time he swayed closer. From across the room, Frank, having observed this, evidently had realized I needed rescuing, for he ambled over and slapped my admirer on the shoulder to get his attention.

When my admirer turned away from me, Frank, "happy" too, inclined his head and seriously confided in his ear, "She talks to flies!" then nonchalantly moseyed away feeling, no doubt, he had done his duty.

With eyes glazed over, my admirer pondered this bizarre morsel of information as he stared after a retreating Frank. I seized the opportunity and made a fast getaway before I could be asked to explain Frank's remark, and wondered if "the fly" would follow me for the rest of my days…and nights.

AUTHOR'S NOTE:

Years later my sister Marty confided her husband, Frank, would never kill a fly after the dinner experience.

I discovered a few years ago *New York Times* writer, John Correy, wrote in *Reader's Digest* about a woman's experience with a fly that followed her from room to room. She, also, talked to the fly and it responded to her directives. It was so similar to my experience. It makes me wonder.

How to Win at the Races

It was Boots' first time at the horse races. Santa Anita was a beautiful racetrack for a first time visit – sun shining on flowers in bloom everywhere one looked, and off in the distance snow-capped mountains. The paddock was filled with million dollar thoroughbred horses, owners, trainers, and the jockeys readying for a run around the track while horseracing fans milled about deciding who the winners might be before placing their bets.

Boots learned to read the racing form, tutored by her friend Alex. He knew a thing or two about racehorses, since he liked, and had been going to the races, since college. Therefore, he had picked the horses they had wagered on in the first few races. Being lucky, they had more winners than losers.

After winning the last race, Boots, now feeling confident and a few bucks richer, said, "Alex, I would like to pick my own horse in the next race."

"Okay, if you wish," he obliged smiling and wished her "good luck" as he buried his nose in his racing form, as did Boots in hers.

Boots studied the racing form, keeping in mind all Alex had explained to her about speed ratings, past performances, along with noting the winning trainers and jockeys – all the while she kept checking the odds. As she did so, Boots observed the water truck wet down the track. Never having seen this happen, she looked on with interest. Then she went back to the racing form. A short time later she hurried to the long line at the betting window. Not a big gambler, she made her bet – two dollars across the board – Win, Place, and Show.

Boots rushed back, clutching her ticket, to join Alex in their box to watch the race, and made it just in time to hear, "The horses are in the gate! They're off!"

The race was on, and soon over. The roaring crowd was overjoyed…and dejected.

Boots jumped up and down…one of the overjoyed. She turned to Alex, "I won! I won! My horse won!"

Alex looked on in shock…one of the dejected. "You won!" he cried unbelieving. "How could you pick *that* horse? He's the longest shot on the board!"

"The form said he likes the mud!" a jubilant Boots informed him, thrilled at winning.

"He likes the mud! You picked him because he liked the mud?" Alex was aghast. "Don't you see the sun shining? It hasn't rained! There is no mud!" he pointed out.

Boots looked at him in wonderment. "Didn't you see the water truck go by wetting the track?"

"What?" The water truck *sprinkled* the track! That's why you bet on the horse?" Alex could only shake his head. Woman's reasoning – how can you beat it? He wouldn't try. Just go on to the next race with a smile. They both picked up their racing forms.

Alex let a few moments pass and without taking his eyes off his racing form, teasing, he said, "Boots, check the track and let me know who you like in the next race."

A not so friendly knuckle punch in the ribs Alex got in reply.

Wake Up! Rebel! The Time Is Now!

The dining table at our house has taken on a different tone and topic these days. One certainly not good for the digestion, but good for letting off steam. Boy, is everyone steamed when the subject of taxes is laid on the table.

There are taxes, and then there are taxes – take a look at your phone bill, your gas bill, your water bill, your electric bill, and how about your cable bill? Shop for clothes, housewares, fill your gas tank, go to the grocery store, dine out, and go to the movies – Tax. Tax. Tax.

"And, oh, how about property tax?" Craig yelled trying to be heard.

Everyone yelled out at once at the mention of tax. Less I forget, the new healthcare tax tacked onto your dining out bill. It's tax, tax, and more tax.

Then, each year there's that universally hated Federal Income Tax, and don't forget State Tax by that dreaded day, April 15th.

I think you get the picture of what is happening at the dinner table these days. It goes on and on. As someone says now every time the news out of Washington comes on TV, they want more spending money, which means more tax money, which brings us to the latest – rumors of a war tax!

"They've got to be kidding!" Barry shouts.

It isn't too long before we're all yelling, "Where is all our hard-earned money going?"

"Nobody knows." But someone explained, "It fell through the cracks."

The government spending really hits a big high as, "Have you heard the latest?" is thrown out there for everyone to chew on. Some reaching high decimals of indignation and disbelief that hit "High C" are too ridiculous not to mention.

For instance:

Have you heard the latest we need to throw our hard-earned money at? To find out why there are obese lesbians. Look around, are we a nation of lesbians? Do we need a study to find out anyone who eats more food than they burn stores it as fat? Nuttier than that, there are shrimp running on treadmills! And mountain lions too! Not overweight people who really need it. Swedish massages for rabbits! Gambling monkeys!

I ask you, is this crazy? Don't Americans get it?

Then the one that almost upturned the table, throwing five billion at getting a bunch of monkeys drunk, so scientists can study the effect of alcohol abuse on their bodies! Getting monkeys smashed! What next?

After everyone at the dinner table offers themselves up as volunteers for the study and vents, the solutions put on the table are at times worse than, "throw the bums out!"

I liked my solution best. I said enough talk. It's time for action.

"Wake Up! Rebel! The time is now! Tell Washington to stop wasting our money. Let's all shout, "No more taxes!" 'til it's heard. Let us get back to real arguing and shouting at the dining table, about the World Series!

"The Super Bowl! The Kentucky Derby! The Masters! The U.S. Open! The American Cup! The cover of the Sports Illustrated!" Loudly, everyone at the table contributes.

"Hey, how about a bit of gossip and laughter!" I say.

"Let's not forget the Victoria Secret Fashion Show!" Dave shouts, reminding us.

I continue shouting, "We mustn't forget the Duluth Trading Company men's "stinky" underwear commercial either!"

Someone else screamed, "And their long tail tees versus the gawking gopher!" and "How about their fire hose work pants against an angry beaver!" Everyone is shouting and laughing.

Duluth's commercials! Now that's something to get excited and shout about over a good ol' spaghetti dinner and a bottle of wine.

Around Our Dinner Table

We never know what subjects will be brought up around the dinner table when our family and friends gather. But, you can be certain that whatever it is, it will be lively. Everybody has a story, especially when it comes to "kooky" friends or relatives. If you look around, you'll discover there's always one who raises your eyebrows, but in a loving way.

We had one. We got her by marriage, once removed. She was a "real" kook. But loveable. She personified the word "kook." When her name was mentioned, it was always with a smile and a question. "What has Jennie done now?"

There were two things that will give you some insight into Jennie – one, she had a lawyer friend.

"Everyone should have a lawyer friend," she advised me one day.

Two, she believed in marriage. She was young, but had been married, I had heard, five times. But when I spoke about her being married five times, I was corrected.

"Five? Where did you get that number? It's seven!" Her nephew corrected me.

When I said, "No wonder she has a lawyer friend with all those divorces."

I was again corrected. "Jennie never got a divorce! She just booted them out!"

One evening, lawyers were brought up at the dinner table, and since her nephew was dining with us, Jennie's latest "escapade" was exposed.

The Witness

Not being able to afford the bus, Jennie hurried down the boulevard to work, deep in worrisome thought – it was her rent as always. It was soon due. She was waitressing, but a toothache and the subsequent dentist bill set her back. She desperately needed some money by the end of the month – her landlady took no excuses, it was pay up or get out. She'd love to get out, but "the dump" as she called it, had been all she could afford that was available. Reaching the corner, she stopped for the light to change before crossing.

The light changed. Jennie put one foot off the curb and suddenly CRASH! BANG! Cars were spinning in all directions. One of the cars involved in the accident careened and came to rest at her feet, barely avoided hitting her as the door flew open.

Without missing a beat, Jennie jumped into the car and strapped on the seatbelt. The young man behind the wheel, dazed and hurt, but not bloodied, cried out bewildered, "What are you doing?"

"Here comes some help, start moaning!" Jennie rapidly hissed. "We're injured! Your neck! Mine! What's your name? I'm your friend, Jennie! Jennie Jerome. — I'M YOUR WITNESS! MOAN!"

Around Our Dinner Table

A friend, Rudy, was a high school teacher and there were many humorous stories told by him. Some came back to bite him in the butt as when talking about art in class one day.

He asked the students if anyone could "name one of the most famous busts in the world."

"But all I got was silence and a giggle or two," he said. "I had expected at least one student to say the ancient Egyptian Queen, Nefertiti, and said so."

Since no one in the class knew who she was, he then proceeded to discuss the Nefertiti bust – who she was, when her bust was created, the sculptor, etc.

Next day the mother of a student called and complained to the principal because he discussed female busts in class and embarrassed her teenage daughter.

Then there was this story Rudy told one evening over dinner around the dining table.

The Rustler

Scotty walked home from school along the rural country road in the Valley kicking the dirt aimlessly with his foot now and again. He wondered if his mother had baked cookies for his afterschool snack. He sure hoped she had made his favorite peanut butter cookies. His mouth watered at the thought. He hurried his steps as he walked along.

Soon he passed by the farmer's field where the milk cow, Bessie, waited and always followed along the fence as Scotty walked on by and talked to her.

However, this day was different. Scotty stopped and, seeing where the fence had been wired together, he undid the wiring and enticed Bessie out. Boy and cow walked together down the country road, he lead the cow with the short dangling rope around her neck on which a bell hung.

When shortly Scotty reached the lane to his house, he turned Bessie around, lightly slapped her on her rump and urged her back home. "Go on now, Bessie, see you tomorrow," he said as he watched her start back up the road. When she stopped and looked around, he again called, "Go on, go on." He continued watching as she ambled off, then turned into his lane. Again, with nothing but peanut butter cookies and milk on his mind, he hurried on home.

When farmer Joe came out to bring Bessie into the barn, she was missing. His eyes scanned the field, but he didn't see her. Disturbed, he walked along the wire fence to locate where she may have escaped and found the opening, which he knew on sight could not have been opened by Bessie.

Farmer Joe returned to the farmhouse and called the sheriff's office. When Sheriff Clark answered he reported his cow, Bessie, missing.

"It seems like the fence had been opened by someone," he explained.

"I'll be on my way, Joe, to take a look." He hung up and reached for his hat.

"Ben," he called to his deputy, "Farmer Joe called. Bessie is missing, probably strayed off somewhere. I'm leaving to check it out."

Shortly he arrived and met Joe at the fence. While they examined the opening, Joe's neighbor, Eddie, cantered up on his horse, stopped, and greeted both men.

"Bess is gone," Joe said, pointing to the fence.

"Oh, I saw Scotty Brown a bit ago walking her down the road," Eddie said. "He was taking her along by the rope around her neck."

Joe and the Sheriff got into the police car and, with Eddie following, they slowly drove down the road to where Eddie had seen Bessie and Scotty. They didn't have to go far before they came upon Bessie alongside the road chewing away.

The next morning, the school was abuzz with the news Scotty Brown was in the town jail – he was charged with cattle rustling. To say Scotty's parents were upset with what had happened was putting it mildly. Scotty was not one who got into trouble.

They had a meeting with farmer Joe, Sheriff Clark, and lawyer Ron George, who was a friend and neighbor. It was a rural neighborhood and all were well-acquainted.

They were also law-abiding citizens. This was not just a schoolboy's prank. Scotty broke a law. What if farmer Joe pressed charges? Scotty's life was in balance. Now a decision had to be made.

Meanwhile, Scotty's homeschool teacher arrived at the jail to see Scotty. Scotty was let out of his cell for the visit.

"Hello, Mr. Marshall," a shamefaced Scotty said.

"Hello, cowboy," Mr. Marshall greeted him smiling. "I brought your books and homework. I don't want you to miss classes."

Scotty was not concerned about homework. Words spilled out of Scotty's mouth in a steady stream, he couldn't talk fast enough.

"You're the only one who has visited me. I didn't rustle Bessie, I just let her out and she walked me home, and I sent her back. It wasn't like I stole her, now everyone's saying I'm a rustler."

"According to the law, you are."

"I'm not!" he insisted on the verge of tears.

At this outburst, Mr. Marshall took it upon himself to explain to Scotty there was an old law in California pertaining to rustling that had never been expunged from the books. "And when you took Bessie through the fence and walked her down the road, you were a rustler," he concluded.

As Mr. Marshall was departing, he left Scotty with something to think about and keep him awake. "Next time, cowboy, if you're going to rustle, make it a herd. One or a hundred, it's all the same verdict."

"What's that?"

"Hanging!"

Around Our Dinner Table

My teens were spent in a small town three miles south of Scranton, PA. It had a Native American name, Minooka. It had a population of about 2,000 people. The school was small and there were small classes. My sister Ruth's class had thirteen students, she recently reminded me, while my high school class was the largest ever with forty students.

Since we were a small town and all the teachers were from the town, they knew some of the students from birth, or were related. Also, some were your neighbors as was ours.

I was very friendly with all my teachers. The principal, I discovered, had a "crush" on and was dating my Aunt Katherine, who lived in Hyde Park. So, I didn't run and hide in the library or put my head in a book to pretend to read like others did if he was seen coming down the hall or dropped in our classroom. I never let on I knew until one day he met me coming out of the library, which was across from his office, and stopped to ask me about her. I never told any of my classmates he was dating my aunt and that was why he always spoke to me. He wasn't from "our town" so he was a stranger, and it was "Yes, sir; no, sir," when you spoke.

My English teacher, born and raised in the town, was also a sportswriter for the Scranton newspaper; I always enjoyed the times walking home with him after school since I aspired to be a newspaper reporter at that young age, and he was encouraging. But, he was only "friendly" outside of class. It was teacher/student once the door was closed and he stood in front of the classroom. Attention and silence, unless you were called upon, prevailed in his class.

Opportunity Lost

My English teacher, Milky Walsh, (yes, that's a nickname, come to think of it, I don't know his first name) gave us an assignment to "write all you know" about a certain subject, and he wrote three subjects on the blackboard with the option of choosing something of our own liking.

I don't recall the three subjects he listed, just that I didn't know anything, or much about any of them, and couldn't think what else I could write about, not that day or any day thereafter, though I thought long and hard. I was a sophomore, fourteen going on fifteen at the time.

The morning arrived to turn in the paper and I didn't have a solitary word written. I was dry.

We were a house full of children, and I hadn't been able to concentrate on the assignment at home. Therefore, I went to school early and persuaded the custodian to let me in so I could write the assignment. I sat at my desk; last seat second row from a wall of open windows that overlooked the back gardens of the houses on the street next to the school. With pen in hand and a blank white sheet of lined paper staring at me, I tried to concentrate on the assignment, but my mind wandered. I stared out the windows and thought what a beautiful day it was.

It was early spring, all was still, the air fresh and a little crisp. There were trees in the gardens and the sun shone brightly, dancing on the new light green leaves, which swayed by a gentle breeze. Bird talk was the only sound that broke the morning silence. I sat at my desk and daydreamed, wishing I wasn't in school facing a white sheet of paper, but outdoors free as the birds.

Although I sat at my desk, my mind and spirit soared, and when it returned, I still didn't have any idea what to write. I couldn't wrap my mind around "write all you know about...." whatever. I really couldn't think of anything I "knew all about."

Since I was confronted with I didn't know "all about" anything, I knew I had to write something because Milky gave us a mark of fifty percent for our daily work, and fifty percent for our written paper. I had always received one hundred in his class. It was acknowledged by all sophomores I was his best student.

Time was running out. Through the second floor open windows I could hear students arriving; their cheerful voices greeting one another; their laughter and calls to each other drowning out the birdsong. Also, breaking into my wandering thoughts despoiling the tranquility of the morning and awakening me to my predicament.

Time had become my enemy.

Desperate I began to write, my pen racing across the blank paper.

I confessed I was not able to complete the assignment because I didn't know "all about" any of the subjects he gave us, and couldn't think of anything else I knew "all about." I described the moments alone with my thoughts on the early spring morn. I recall I purposely decided to put in a sentence with a semicolon, and one with an exclamation point, and another sentence with a question mark.

The bell rang.

The rest of the class trooped in and dropped their assignment on Milky's desk, as per directive, before they took to their seats. I had just finished writing, the shortest time it ever took me to write anything, when Milky entered the classroom and I rushed up the aisle, trying to beat him to his desk.

I didn't.

But without a glance in my direction, he let me put my paper on top of the pile he had gathered in his hands.

I was wrung out by this time and decided on the spot I didn't like deadlines. So all thoughts I ever had of becoming a newspaper reporter flew right out of my head. Never to return.

I wondered through the rest of the day about my mark because I had two short paragraphs only – well, short for me – I didn't fill a page as I recall, and I hadn't even had time to edit. No hundred for me this month, I was certain.

That night while lying in bed before sleep overtook me, I had a revelation. I realized what I should have written, and then wondered whether it would have been worth risking zero on my paper.

What I should have written was:

I didn't know everything about anything. Sign my name, add P.S. And want credit.

How I wish I had the revelation earlier and the courage I now had in hindsight to write that. Oh, how I wish I did! I often think of the opportunity lost by fate.

Nevertheless, I received fifty percent for my paper, one hundred percent for the month. I was shocked and thrilled to pieces by the unexpected mark, and took it without question.

Many months later, Milky confided, as we walked home together after school, I was writing beyond my age. He surprised me by adding I was the only student he ever had who turned in a paper relating to a stream of consciousness that also had a sentence having a semicolon, and another having an exclamation point, and yet another sentence ending with a question mark.

I laughed to myself, for I immediately knew the paper to which he was referring, remembered the fifty percent he gave me and chalked one up to daydreaming and punctuation marks.

I was so busy congratulating myself for deliberately including punctuation marks that paid off I didn't take the opportunity presented to confront Milky about the assignment.

Still today, there are times I mentally kick myself for not challenging him about "write all you know" when the opportunity stared me in the face.

The Rose Bowl

It was New Year's Day in California. That meant, along with hangovers, the Rose Parade and the Rose Bowl in Pasadena. The California sun shone brightly and there was a breeze blowing off the snow-capped San Gabriel Mountains, putting a chill in the air. It was a glorious California winter day, perfect for playing football.

The Rose Bowl was filling for the football game, and all about chatter and laughter rose from the crowd. Everyone was in the highest of spirits. Marching bands were tuning up, adding to the excitement and anticipation filling the air. Some football fans, lucky enough to get tickets, had already filled the stadium. Strangers spoke to strangers while taking their seats.

"You look like you were a football player," Mary Lou observed as the bulky hunk sat down next to her.

"Yeah, that was my game," he acknowledged with a remembering smile.

"Oh, really! What position did you play?" she asked with interest.

"Tight end," he replied.

"Did you ever play in the Rose Bowl?"

"Naw, we didn't make it the year I played." He sounded disappointed.

"My husband played in the Rose Bowl one year," Mary Lou revealed with pride.

"Oh, he did!" he exclaimed, perking up. "What position did he play?"

"Piccolo," Mary Lou proclaimed with a twinkle in her eye and a laugh in her voice.

He didn't even smile.

Our Proud New American

Starbucks! Where is the cleaner? Wasn't that where the cleaner was? I looked around the mini mall. It had been newly landscaped, and there were new black wrought iron arm chairs and round tables with maroon sun umbrellas scattered on the walkway fronting the stores.

I walked along the row of stores. I was looking for our shoemaker; I needed lifts on my heels, but all I found was pizza, Chinese, and Mexican food next to a French restaurant, and a new hamburger restaurant where formerly we always had the best spaghetti. Surprisingly the high-end boutique was still there sandwiched between the candy store, except now, it was "The Candy Shoppe." But no shoemaker.

What happened in the months I was in the desert? I wondered as I looked around at all the changes and, feeling like a lost child, I retraced my steps. I bought a latte in Starbucks and a chocolate croissant from the new French Boulangerie, and sat at a table under the new sun umbrella in front of Starbucks enjoying my snack and coffee while I regrouped.

All my plans for dropping off my shoes and going on my way had gone up in smoke. I checked my to-do list to see what else I had to do while here and found "drugstore." I looked across the parking lot and saw it was still there sandwiched between the bank and the hardware store. When I saw "fill gas tank" reminder and looked toward the opposite corner where the gas station had always been, to my amazement, there was a new one-story building with Chase Bank – "Bank" in big bold letters on its side. Now I really felt disoriented. How could our gas station, that had been there forever, become a bank in eight months? If it was not nine o'clock in the morning, I'd thought Starbucks put more than coffee in their paper cups.

It certainly was busy – cars parking, young people jumping out, striding by, going into Starbucks for their morning coffee engrossed in their iPods, weaving through the tables and chairs without looking. It was fascinating to see as they returned with a latte in one hand and a phone in the other while they raced back into their pickups, convertibles, or black window cars I didn't recognize the make. No one touched a chair, tripped on the curb, or bumped into another like them. They all must have had radar to navigate through the tables and chairs without mishap. This morning rush hour was new to me. I certainly rolled out the wrong side. I contemplated going home, jumping back into bed, and getting out the other side when I was startled out of my thoughts by shouting.

"Boots, is that you? I thought you were in Rancho Mirage?" It was an old schoolmate, Camielle.

"Hi! No, I've been here for a week. One hundred ten degrees in the shade told me it was time to leave the desert."

Camielle pulled a chair and sat down after putting her latte and cell phone on the table. The huge black leather bag with brass buckles, studs, and fringe that looked like it weighed a ton without anything in it slung over her shoulder, she put on another chair.

I couldn't help but remark, "What are you carrying in that bag?"

Camielle laughed good-naturedly. "All my worldly goods. I don't know what I'll pull out when I put my hand in. I know I'd be embarrassed to turn it over, and even if someone offered me a million to see what was in it, I'd have to decline. It's my office too."

"I don't know why I asked. I have two bags – a tote I never leave home without. I'm prepared for a rainstorm, gale, blizzard, even an earthquake," I elaborated. "Look at everybody with their backpacks, huge shoulder bags, and fanny packs; it looks like they are all running away from home!

They both laughed at the scene – the fairer sex and their bags.

"How's everyone? The family? I've been so busy, I haven't kept in touch. I'm even a stranger in my own home," Camielle confessed.

"If I start to tell you, we'll be here all day. Let's just say everyone's well, but if we hear the paramedics speeding by, I'll be checking my cell." I laughed.

"Then I won't tell you about my aches and pains – my arthritis, my knees are killing me."

"Join the club."

Camielle was in Real Estate and the one person who knew everyone. I was aware by the end of the day everyone in the neighborhood she talked to would know I'm up from the desert for the summer. So, I better get on with my to-do's I had planned for the day before we started dishing the dirt. Save it for another time. I had too much to do, so I said, "I came here to drop some shoes at the shoemaker..."

"Oh, he's been gone forever," Camielle interrupted waving to a friend, and then added, "No more 'Flowers by Uncle Steve' either."

"Not Uncle Steve! What will we do for flowers? I see the gas station is gone," I groaned.

"Yeah, there's only one now, and don't look for Denny's; it's going to be another bank."

"Another bank! How many do we need?" I laughed. "Please say that Hi-Time is still there. I would hate to have Tracy and Keith gone too."

"So would I. Tracy's still there. I was in to see her yesterday."

"Good to hear. I'll drop by to let her know I'm in town. But I need a shoemaker. Please tell me there is a shoemaker in town."

"No and yes," Camielle laughed. "Our shoemaker was located in a high rent district, and when his lease was up the rent went up, so he left. But I found another shoemaker, if you don't mind a little driving." Rummaging in her bag as she spoke, Camielle produced her card case and handed me a card. "Tell him I sent you."

I looked at the card. "Oh, I know where this is. Great."

I stood and, gathering up my empty cup, paper plate, and soiled napkins, tossed them into the trash. "I'd better go over before he disappears too, like all the other old landmarks."

Camielle and I hugged and, after promising to get together soon, we picked up our carryall bags and went our separate ways.

I located the little shoemaker shop Camille recommended. No one was in the shop except a small man working on a shoe. He looked up when I entered. His Asian face lit up and he greeted me warmly with a broad smile. His was such a happy face, it made me smile back.

"My lady, how I help you?" he greeted. There was even a smile in his welcoming voice.

"I sure hope you can. I have some heels I want repaired." I pulled my shoes out of the large tote, and put them on the counter that separated us.

He picked them up, examined them one by one with a few "hmm, hmm's," then replied, "No prob-lem. I can fix. Very nice shoes."

I watched him examining my two hundred dollar slippers. He kept smiling, admiring, hmming, and finally finished examining the slippers. He again said, "Very nice. Nice."

"Good. When can I have them?" I asked.

"When you need? Not tomorrow."

"How about the end of the week?"

"End of week good."

He asked my name for the ticket, and smiling broadly he found my name "Boots" amusing. "You name, girl name shoes."

We completed the shoe transaction and I watched as he ticketed them and put them aside, giving me my half of the ticket.

As I put it in my purse, I politely asked his name.

"Joey," he answered rather proudly.

"Joey!" That's not an Asian name," I remarked.

"No, no, no, not Asian! I'm 'merican." He pointed to the American flag on the wall.

I looked at the flag, and then noticed he also had a photo of the President. His t-shirt was also red and white-striped with a navy blue apron covering navy blue trousers. Again, he repeated, "I'm 'merican, 'merica land of the free."

Now it was my turn to "hmmm, hmmm" as I took it all in.

Joey continued to explain. "When I come 'merica, man ask me I go church. I say no know church. He take me church St. Joseph. I go church Joseph and now I am Joey. I'm 'merican. So 'merican name." As I took all this information in, he asked, "You new in neighborhood?"

"No," I replied. "But I live nearby."

He nodded in understanding. Curious, I asked his nationality.

"'Merican." He seemed to grow taller as he stated it.

"You are…I mean what country did you come from?"

"I here Vietnam. I'm 'merican."

Every time he said he was an American, he seemed to glow and grow another inch.

"By the way, Camielle gave me your card."

"Ah, I know Cami," he said smiling. "Cami she send. Cami nice."

Turning to go, I said, "Goodbye, American Joey." Leaving him with a smiling face, a glow, and I swear another inch taller, this very proud American.

As I made my way to my car, I wondered how he came by the name "Joey" instead of "Joseph" from St. Joseph's church. I must remember to ask "'merican Joey" when I came back to pick up my shoes.

Perhaps I might tell him how I'm "Boots": Girl named shoes. But, I wonder since he was Joey, and Camielle was Cami, whether I will be Bootsie.

Around Our Dinner Table

Everyone I know is either a cat lover or a dog lover. There are more cats and dogs around here than there are children, except when school is not in session, and the children are across the street in the park playing soccer, baseball, on the swings, flying kites weather permitting, or just running around, chasing each other.

Early morning is the best time for dogs; it's like a dog show – all the dog walkers, with more than one leash. I saw one with seven leashes! Dragging her along. All colors and breeds, which I must confess some I don't know, but they are running along, some straining on leashes, but all stopping and, as my little niece use to say, "Doing their business."

The cats are seen later, walking along the fence, jumping to the garage next door, and then from there to the house rooftop that's a daily ritual. Another neighborhood cat comes by after lunch daily and lies near the front planter for about an hour or two, while another does the same in the back garden, except she, or he, curls up for a snooze on one of the wicker chair cushions.

So there are many, many animal tales wagged at our dinner table.

My friend Laurie is a cat lover, as well as dogs, and all animals lover. She's always had a cat. For many, many years, we've exchanged the same cat Christmas card. She sends it to me and it goes back to her after New Year, and I expect it again when the next Christmas comes around.

Thirty Years Ago and Three Thousand Miles Away

Laurie couldn't be happier as she greeted her sister, Jonny, and her three teen daughters as they ran into her open arms. She dropped her suitcase, did a twirly embrace with the children, and air kissed her sister over their heads. They had come to the airport to welcome her as she hadn't visited Maine in a few years.

"Let me see you!" she cried as she released the girls and stepped back to look at them. "My how you've grown! You're young ladies!" Turning to her sister, she asked, "Where did the children go?"

The young girls preened and brightened up, quickly checking to see if their mother took note. They had been trying to convince her they were no longer children, but it was like talking to the wall. Now that they had Aunt Laurie visiting, maybe she'd listen and change her mind. They looked at each other, crossed fingers, and exchanged smiles.

"Let me carry your suitcase," Rebecca said reaching out.

"I'll carry your tote, Aunt Laurie," chirped Kate taking the tote from Laurie.

"I've nothing to carry," moaned Laura.

"Why don't you carry her?" Kate teased.

"You're not funny!" Laura retorted giving Kate a not so gentle push.

There was laughter all around as they wound their way through the crowded airport terminal heading for their SUV parked in the "Loading Zone."

After the more than a three thousand mile air trip from Southern California, Laurie took a few days just lounging around unwinding from her hectic work schedules. She had been working without a vacation except for a few holiday weekends spent at the cabin in Big Bear with friends, or getaway weekends with them in Palm Springs. Now with her family surrounding her, Laurie felt relaxed and rested. There was something about the farm in Maine, the air, the expanse of green meadows, and the forest of trees, Laurie had always found refreshing in mind, body, and spirit like no other place she had ever been.

The days went by in a whirl.

After Laurie had her fill of the Maine lobster, clams, or clam chowder it was always heavenly to sit on the garden swing with Jonny and reminisce about their youth and family.

"Do you remember the kittens I had when a child, Jonny?" Laurie asked as she cuddled and scratched their old tomcat purring contentedly in her arms.

"Do you mean the two you and James found and claimed as your own?"

"Yeah."

"What were their names? I forgot. It was so long ago, I don't remember."

"It was long ago – about forty years long ago!" Laurie agreed. "Forty years!" No wonder I don't remember. What were their names?" Jonny asked again.

"Their names were Petey and Petunia."

"How could I forget Petunia?" Jonny laughed, hitting her forehead with her palm.

"Well, I never did," Laurie revealed. "All through my life, I've often thought of them. Whenever I think of James, I think of us playing with the kittens as children."

Laurie and Jonny had a fun time swinging and remembering the cats' antics, especially Petunia's, and all the subsequent pets they had were thought of and brought joyful memories too.

"But I always remembered Petey and Petunia most of all," Laurie said wistfully.

The shrill ringing of the phone interrupted and Jonny bolted into the house to answer.

Returning to the doorway she called out, "That was my friend Lilly from the farm across the road, inviting us over for some freshly baked cherry pie and ice tea."

"Cherry pie! My favorite!" At the mention of cherry pie, Laurie had already jumped up off the swing and raced across the lawn. "You did tell her we'd be on our way, didn't you?" she cried.

"I think I did mention it." Jonny laughed.

They left a note for the girls telling them where they were and locked up, and, as when children, arm in arm they gaily hurried down the lane, across the road to the neighboring farm and the waiting goodies.

Conversation over the cherry pie touched on what their neighbors did and their farm animals.

Then Jonny remarked, "Laurie has something in common with you, Lilly. Laurie also is a small animal lover, and has always been since childhood."

"Really, then you must meet some of mine. Come, let's go."

Lilly was only too happy to walk them out to the one hundred year old red barn at the rear of the house, right out of a Grandma Moses painting that housed all her small pets.

They crossed a meadow blooming with buttercups and Queen Anne's lace on a road that led into the old red barn. A number of cats, mousers more than likely, were lying around as well as playing, and a number of chickens strutted about and pecked as they entered the huge barn.

Laurie and Jonny followed Lilly walking around as she greeted each pet with a word or two. Suddenly, she stooped and picked up a huge angora rabbit, turned, and thrust it into Laurie's waiting arms.

Laurie's face lit up with happiness. It was love at first sight. The Angora rabbit was one big gorgeous fluff. Soon Angora fur was shed all over Laurie, even reaching her face and mouth as she snuggled it closer.

Lilly approached, cuddling yet another huge Angora rabbit and she, too, was soon covered with shedding Angora fur. But she didn't seem to mind either. They were her adored pets.

"What are their names?" Laurie asked brushing wisps of Angora out of her mouth at the same time.

Laughing at Laurie and the shedding Angora rabbit, Lilly lovingly replied, "The one I'm holding is Petey, and you're holding Petunia."

Startled, both Laurie and Jonny's eyes flew open wide in surprise and disbelief.

Stunned, Laurie stuttered, "Wh-wh-what did you say?"

"This is Petey, and you're holding Petunia," Lilly repeated.

As the names hit her again, Laurie's knees buckled and she slowly folded to the board floor, still clutching Petunia to her breast.

Forty years later and three thousand miles she had travelled and unbelievably discovered another Petey and Petunia in an old red barn on a farm in Maine.

Mary Christmas

Shari planned to spend Christmas holidays with her sister in Bermuda, and since World War Two was not over, she had a problem at the LaGuardia Airport in New York City leaving the country.

She stood in line while the ticket agent processed each passenger, wishing them: "Have a nice stay, Merry Christmas," as he finished and handed them their ticket.

Finally, Shari reached the ticket agent.

"Where are you going?" the ticket agent inquired.

"Bermuda."

"Why are you going to Bermuda?"

"For a visit."

"Who will you be visiting?"

"My sister."

"What is your sister's name?"

"Mary Christmas."

"Merry Christmas," he repeated.

"What is your sister's name?" he asked again.

"Mary Christmas."

"Merry Christmas," he once more repeated.

"Now, tell me, what is your sister's name?"

"Mary Christmas."

"Excuse me," he said and made a hasty retreat.

Soon another agent arrived and took his place. He smiled at Shari, then said, "You are visiting your sister in Bermuda, is that correct?"

"Yes."

"What is your sister's name?"

"Mary Christmas."

"Merry Christmas," he repeated.

"Yes," she said.

"Yes what?"

"Mary Christmas."

"Merry Christmas," he said again.

By this time, Shari had enough of this. "Yes," she said. "My sister lives in Bermuda. She is married to a soldier named Sgt. Francis Christmas. Her name is Mary Christmas. M-a-r-y Christmas," she spelled.

The red faced ticket agent quickly processed her ticket and as he handed it to her, instead of wishing her, "Have a nice stay, Merry Christmas," as the agents had been wishing each former passenger farewell, he said, "Have a nice stay, Happy New year!"

The Proposal

I hadn't seen my brother, Jon, for some time. So on the way to visit my sister, I decided to stop by and say "hello" to him since he lived only a stone's throw away from her condominium at the Marina where I was heading for the weekend.

Upon arriving, I greeted his wife then asked, "Is Jon home?"

"He's outside, sitting under the tree with a friend who stopped by. Go on out. He'll be happy to see you."

"I'll just yell a 'hello.' Let's all have dinner either tonight or tomorrow night."

"Tonight sounds good to me."

I went out on the patio, called and waved, "Hi, Jon! See you later!" Jon rose from his chair, dumping "Ugly" off his lap, and beckoned, "Come say hello."

Seeing his guest rise too, not wanting to be rude, I went to the back garden and Jon introduced me to his friend, Sam.

Though not bad on the looks, he wasn't anyone I would have expected to be a friend of my brother, so well appointed, he was just the opposite of Jon. With his dark wavy hair, deep tan, Sam was muscled football player turned yachtsman dressed in a navy Lauren knit sport shirt opened at his throat, creased white trousers and navy topsiders. He looked "edgy" and, unexpectedly, oozed danger – maybe it was his bulk and eyes hidden behind dark sunglasses that gave that impression. While on the other hand, Jon, I must say, is quite good-looking and very approachable. In his faded cutoffs and t-shirt blazoned with the latest "craze" that was slightly tattered, along with sporty sandals covering his feet instead of knocked off nearby, he looked, well, not too shabby, just "comfortable." Oh yes, Jon either had his dog, "Ugly," or his cat,

"Cat," sitting on him, curled around or following him. Notwithstanding their dissimilar choice of California beach attire, I discovered later they were summa cum laude college friends who were intellectually attuned which explained the friendship.

After refusing an offered, "Cool lemonade?" and with a polite "Nice meeting you," to Sam, and "See you at dinner tonight," to Jon, I ran along.

That was how I met Sam.

Shortly, Jon called. "You have an admirer. After you left, Sam's first words were, 'you didn't tell me you had another sister,' and he accused me of hiding you." Laughing, he added, "He came by to tell me he was getting married soon and wants me to be in the wedding party."

"Oh, that's nice. Tux?"

"You bet. Shoes too," he tossed in.

"Are you also going to wear a pinkie ring?" I needled.

"Oh, you noticed his ring!" I could tell he was swallowing a laugh. "How could I miss it?" I came back at him.

I saw Sam once again for a fast few minutes while shopping at the mall and he amazed me by handing me his card and asking me to call him if anyone gave me any problems, and he'd take care of it.

Jon laughed when I told him. He teased, "Well, if you need a bodyguard or want to give someone a broken nose, call him."

"That's not funny," I said, even though I did think it mighty strange indeed.

It wasn't long before I received an invitation to Sam's wedding – surprising me again, and I discussed attending with Jon. During our conversation, he disclosed Sam had continued to stop by, "Probably hoping you'd be visiting, and always had a question about you." He urged me to attend, saying, "We'll all be there," even though I didn't know the bride and barely knew Sam.

The wedding day soon arrived. Saturday being the wedding, I was leaving Friday night for the Marina, and as I picked up my dress bag, tote, and wedding gift I had placed at the door, the phone rang. I wasn't going to answer, but decided I'd better, just in case it was something I needed to bring along with me.

To my utter surprise, it was Sam!

"This is your last chance to marry me."

"WHAT?"

"We could fly to Las Vegas tonight!"

"Aren't you the one getting married tomorrow?"

"It's your last chance! I need an answer - NOW!"

Tonight was wedding rehearsals and a dinner I had learned from my brother who was to attend, since he was in the wedding party. I was astonished by the call since I had only seen this man twice, for minutes.

But I was not too stunned to tell him, "I'm leaving for the Marina. I don't want to get hung up in Friday night traffic. I've really no time to talk. Bye," and hung up. I didn't want to confront "the proposal" and get into a long conversation with Sam about his wedding tomorrow that, I'm assuming from his call, is in trouble or perhaps called off. I'd soon find out.

I again picked up my dress bag, tote, and wedding gift and was out the door. That evening no one gave any indication the wedding was off. So, I kept the unusual "proposal call" to myself.

The next morning, I decided to give the wedding a pass and only attend the reception. I couldn't sit and listen to someone "Love, Honor, and Obey" after I got that weird proposal from him the night before.

I easily went through the receiving line with others without incident, and then gorged on the delicious canapés while I sipped a glass of bubbly as I mingled. With the great number of wedding guests, I was able to disappear before the toasts and cake cutting without it being noticed I slipped out. I did so because I tried avoiding a private face-to-face with the groom. What could I say? What could he say? I felt it was better to make a getaway rather than have what could only be an uncomfortable encounter. At least on my part.

Later that evening, I called my brother wanting to know if he had given Sam my telephone number, and astounded him when I told him about the outlandish call. We discussed the weird proposal in the form of an ultimatum, and we both had the same thought – who in his right mind would call and propose an elopement to his friend's sister on the night before he was scheduled to marry someone else? What girl in her right mind would accept it from a stranger? Didn't Sam understand that? We both marveled, but couldn't solve the mystery of the outrageous call, or the timing since Jon was aware the evening before at rehearsals and dinner, Sam had behaved much like a man looking forward to his wedding day. This was after calling and proposing we elope to Las Vegas!

One thing I did learn from speaking to Jon, however, was Sam had asked him if he believed in love at first sight after we had met in the garden, but Jon thought he was referring to the girl he intended to marry.

I asked Jon to keep "the proposal" under his hat. I really didn't have to ask, he was just as anxious as I to keep it to ourselves; we felt no need to embarrass the bride.

Three months passed then Sam became the hot topic of conversation. He was either getting an annulment or getting a divorce. No one knew, so I called his friend, my brother. He was no help. He hadn't seen nor heard from Sam since the wedding. He was completely in the dark.

Then my sister met one of his ex-girlfriends, one we all liked, on the dock and learned Sam was, again, staying with her but they weren't socializing.

We didn't see Sam, and he didn't drop by to visit my brother. Finally, we heard he was no longer married nor living at the Marina, but had bought a house in a beach town south along the Pacific coast.

A few months later, Sam was, again, the hot topic of conversation. Sam was discovered dead in his home from a massive heart attack. We were all shocked. Also found in his home was one million dollars in a suitcase under his bed. This brought on a bigger shock to everyone.

I immediately called my brother upon hearing the news. He knew why I was calling.

"Drugs!" I said.

"No! Sam would never have anything to do with drugs!"

"Then what? Who has a million dollars under their bed in a suitcase?"

"The guy who wanted you to elope to Las Vegas the night of his wedding rehearsal to marry someone else? The same one who asked you to promise if you had any problems with anyone, you were to call him, and he'd take care of it."

"Well, I know you told me he was a bodyguard to very wealthy people, but ONE MILLION UNDER THE BED?"

"It is a puzzlement." Jon was silent for a moment, then, in what was his Rhett Butler voice, he said, "Just think, Scarlett – you could have been a rich widow!"

I groaned, "Good-BYE, Jon!" while he laughed. I quickly hung up before the discussion could get more bizarre.

Scarlett is my name, courtesy of my mother who was watching a rerun of *Gone with the Wind* when I decided to make my debut into this world. Bringing forth his Rhett Butler routine at a time like this! How irreverent could my brother get?

But I knew that wasn't the end. No need now for secrets. I had a strong feeling along with "the million dollars in a suitcase under the bed" that "the proposal" would be the buzz when we gathered at the dinner table for our planned "fish and chips" get together that night.

And I wasn't wrong.

Daylight Robbery

Martha stopped by Marshall's to pick up a few needed items. She paid for them, and the clerk asked, "Do you want a bag?"

What a strange question. "Yes, please," Martha replied rather perplexed.

"That will be ten cents," the clerk said as she put the items in the plastic bag.

"Ten cents?" Martha questioned.

"Yes, ten cents."

"Ten cents," Martha repeated.

"Yes, for the bag. Ten cents."

"Let me understand this," Martha said, unbelieving, "you want ten cents for the bag to put the items in that I just spent fifty dollars on."

"Yes, the bag is ten cents."

Martha couldn't carry out the items she had purchased without a bag, so she ponied up the ten cents, grumbling all the time.

As she walked to her car, still annoyed about the ten cent charge for the bag, she noticed a young man coming toward her – over his arm was a couple pair of trousers with tags dangling.

She stopped him and said, "Excuse me, but are you returning those pants?"

He looked at her leery about where this conversation was going, and said rather hesitantly, "Yes."

"The reason why I'm asking was because you don't have them in a bag."

"Oh, they didn't give me one. They wanted ten cents for a bag, so I didn't buy one. I didn't have time to try them on, so I took them home, and now I'm returning them."

"Well, I was wondering because they just charged me ten cents for this bag to carry out what I bought for fifty dollars."

"I didn't buy one," he repeated, walking away.

As Martha turned to continue to her car, she noticed another man approaching, carrying over his arm boxer shorts, t-shirts, and socks. "I guess you didn't buy a bag," she remarked.

He started laughing. "I wasn't going to pay ten cents for a plastic bag that cost them about three cents. I wasn't going to be ripped off!" He continued to his BMW.

Martha was still smarting about the ten cent plastic bag when she sat down at the dinner table. When Ruth arrived for dinner and asked what she was so riled about, Martha told her about the ten cent bag rip off.

Ruth exclaimed, "Ten cents! You were lucky. I was in the 99 cent store and bought several items, and when I reached the cashier, she asked me if I had a bag. I told her I didn't – that I don't carry around plastic grocery bags.

'Would you like one?' she asked.

I looked at all I had purchased – there was no way I could carry them without a bag and said, 'Yes.'

She bagged my purchases and said, 'That will be 99 cents.'

I said, 'What for?'

'For the bag,' she told me.

'What bag?' I asked.

'The one I put the groceries in,' she said.

I said, '99 cents for the bag!'

She said, 'This is a 99 cent store. Everything in the store is 99 cents.'"

"I guess I was lucky I shopped at a store where the bags were ten cents," Martha said, laughing for the first time since she arrived.

Around Our Dinner Table

Shirley wasn't her name. "What was it?" you ask.
I never did know. Nor did anyone else.

All anyone knew was as a child she didn't like her name, so she changed it to Shirley, and thereafter would only answer to that name. So, she became Shirley to everyone, but me.

I first met Shirley at a party one Saturday night. Actually, we came late to the party, and by that time the party could only be called a drunken brawl. She was the least intoxicated, or so I thought at the time. But there was instant rapport. We were two entirely different personalities that somehow clicked despite the fact I would be considered demure in comparison to her flamboyancy.

Though she was dismissed by most as out of step with the rest of the world, but never an airhead, I recognized her depths and found much about her to be admired. In time, I discovered she had no close friends but many acquaintances, and these were mainly drinking buddies she only associated with at the bars she frequented.

It was some time after we had become acquainted that when speaking about her, I became aware I was referring to her as, "my friend Shirley," and then it became more apparent when anyone mentioning her to me invariably said, "your friend Shirley."

And so, our friendship began and bloomed.

My Friend Shirley

My friend Shirley had called.

"Meet me at the Deli for lunch," she said and disconnected. This request was unusual because we met each day of the week for lunch at the Deli.

All morning I wondered what the unusual call was all about. She worked at a television station and I worked at a movie studio in Hollywood, which had a commissary. But we only ate at the studio commissary when we were entertaining guests so they could tell all their friends they ate at the table next to movie stars who were lunching in the commissary, which most did. Therefore, the call was bewildering.

At noon I sat in a booth at the Deli watching the door, waiting for my friend Shirley to put in an appearance. You always knew when she arrived anywhere for she made an entrance. She was model tall – lanky, all long arms and legs, very good looking. Her light brown hair, bleached by the California sun that always seemed to be combed by the wind, framed a smiling face.

There she was, swinging through the door, seeking me, and loping over to the booth with a cheery "Hi!" to everyone seated she knew and passed on the way. "Did you order for me?" she asked slipping into the booth, knowing full well that I had.

"Yeah," I said anyway. Whoever arrived first, ordered. We've been eating together so long now, we'd eat what was put in front of us by Lucy, our waitress, and like it too, regardless who ordered.

With a deep sigh, Shirley dropped her large shoulder bag next to her on the seat. I always said I wanted her to will it to me. It was so heavy, I just knew she had to keep all of her valuables in there. As with everything else she owned, it was the latest designer bag.

Bag discarded, she plunged right in, "You've got to help me out."

Here we go again, I wasn't surprised. She was in a jam at least once a month. Though, this I knew had to be serious because of the phone call to make certain we'd do lunch.

"What is it this time?" I ventured.

"My mother called last night."

Oh, heck. These calls from her mother always spelled trouble for Shirley.

"She called last week, what is she on you for now?" I dared ask.

"Nothing," she said, then rushed on, "she's coming to town and she wants me to have dinner with her."

"So, get gussied up and have dinner with her." It's only a dinner I thought and pushed. "What's so bad about a couple of hours, even if she ragged you all through dinner, it's a free meal?" Shirley wasn't that flush she could turn down a dinner invitation, even if it was her mother.

"I will." Exasperated, Shirley continued, "She wants to meet my friends. She asked me to bring a friend along." She took on a more serious tone. "You have to come with me. It's Friday night."

Well, that explained the call.

"Why me? You have other friends," I hedged.

"Yeah. But you're the only one who wears a little black dress, and also wears pearls. She'd approve of you." She laughed, and I ignored both – the dig and the laugh.

Then, looking across the table at me square in the face, she asked, "Seriously, can you imagine me taking Ginger to meet my mother? Her flaming red hair with a pink streak? In a dress that looks like a flower garden in full bloom?"

I had to laugh at the picture she painted as she continued. "I've told you enough about my mother to know she'd have men in white jackets come for me and haul me north."

"Friday night? Where is she taking us?" I wondered aloud.

"Perinos – where else?"

Perinos was not just eating out. Perinos was Dining! With a big "D."

"Do you have anything to wear?" I questioned.

Shirley had a closet full of designer clothes, but I didn't know what was in the cleaners or was in condition to pass her mother's inspection.

She assured me she had. "A box arrived a few days ago with a new dress," Shirley informed me. "I should have known she'd be coming to town and planned to have dinner with me."

It figured.

I knew my friend Shirley hated the dressed up, on best behavior, formal dinners with her mother. The request to meet her friends I could tell was really bugging her, though I noted she didn't seem to mind enough taking me along to suffer an evening under scrutiny by "mother."

I brought it to her attention, as I agreed to help her out.

I was my friend Shirley's only acquaintance she spoke to about her mother and revealed her relationship with her. She early on felt she could trust me with all her hidden feelings about her family, and a mother's dominance from which she was running away.

Shirley was an only child, extremely intelligent, who excelled in sports and anything else she tried. She played the piano like no other. Whenever I hear the Warsaw Concerto, I always remember the night she finally decided to convince me she had been forced to take piano lessons since early childhood, shocking everyone in the room to silent attention when she played it for me. At the last note, there was complete silence, then boisterous applause. She was that good.

Shirley was now studying jazz piano and her boogie-woogie was top of the heap. Of course, her mother was fronting the money. She thought, since Shirley's first recital as a child, Shirley would one day be a concert pianist. Little did she know her daughter was silently rebelling, and sat in at clubs playing jazz for her own entertainment. All hell would break loose if she only knew where the piano lesson money was going, for Shirley was the obedient child when with "mother."

Her father, who was a very successful, wealthy, small tool manufacturer, and her mother were divorced when she was a young child. What I gathered from Shirley, her mother was a very bitter woman who did not allow her father to see her after the divorce. Therefore, Shirley never referred to having a father she didn't know.

After the divorce, he remarried and had other children, who Shirley did not know either. They never met. When asked, she always referred to herself an "only child."

To have something to do after her divorce, her mother acquired a position as a buyer for a high-end dress shop she had frequented when married. Shirley confided they were happy to have her because she had "taste and style." It wasn't too long after several buying trips with the owner of the store they moved in together. Child Shirley was moved out.

From that time on, Shirley lived at a boarding school. She never lived in a home with her mother again. After graduating college, she was still on her own with an allowance until she began to work. Once she was earning her own money, she moved out of her mother's shadow but never out of her life completely.

Her mother and her friend never married, though they lived together for years. During that period, Shirley saw him and her mother only occasionally when she was called to meet at a restaurant for dinner. He was always very cordial, but they were strangers as throughout his life she rarely saw him. When he died, Shirley's mother inherited and became the owner of their high-end fashionable woman's store, and she kept Shirley very well-dressed.

Shirley, who loved casual sport clothes, had a closet full of high-style designer dresses, suits, coats, scarves her mother replenished each season and Shirley took to a discount store when she was in need of cash, but smart enough to keep a few items for when her mother made an unexpected visit to Southern California. She never visited Shirley's home nor Shirley hers. Since childhood, Shirley met and visited with her mother, when called, at a formal dinner in a restaurant.

So, now here we were, preparing once again for "a visit." I've never been intimidated by anyone, and certainly not by my mother since a very early age, but Shirley was a nervous wreck. She assured me I'd understand after I spent the evening with her mother. I expected her to be critical, but I didn't expect her to be as bad as Shirley was making out.

All conversation for the next few days with Shirley concerned the dinner and her mother. "Al, I've got to have a haircut and I need a manicure badly. And, by the way, do you have a handkerchief I could borrow? God forbid if I have to sneeze and pull out a Kleenex – and, oh, how about bringing your Chanel 5 – she'll be sure to recognize the smell."

That request did it for me.

"I can't put that bottle in my evening bag!" I cried. I'd had just about enough of the blasted dinner....mother....and Shirley.

"Just bring it, she insisted, we'll leave it in the car."

"This is all about you – what about me?" I protested. "I am the one going to be under the microscope. I'm trying on and rejecting everything in my wardrobe."

I didn't want to let Shirley down, and was beginning to wonder if I had made a mistake going along with her. I didn't need her mother or Shirley to drive me nuts over a dinner in a high-end restaurant.

"Just put on your black dress and your pearls and sandals; she'll adopt you." Shirley dismissed me, ignoring my outburst.

She was so unhinged by the visit I finally stopped taking her calls until the fateful evening.

My friend Shirley did not exaggerate when she briefed me on what to expect when I met her mother. She did not personify the word "mother." She was statuesque. Cold. My immediate thought was "Ice Queen." She looked like a mature dress model who had just stepped out of a Saks Fifth Avenue window, perfectly coiffed – her manner suggested no breeze would dare blow a hair out of place. Unlike her daughter, Shirley, who always looked as if a breeze had been playing with her hair.

Shirley was right on about her mother and the "Chanel 5" perfume. I immediately picked up on it when I observed the slight twitch of her nose. I had never been "sniffed" before and found it amusing this reserved, haughty person could be caught doing so, and judged us by the result.

Afterward, we thought the dinner was a huge success for Shirley, and I passed her scrutiny and questioning. Shirley knew what was coming and, since I was briefed, we had all the right answers. At times I thought I would burst from holding the laughter building up inside me, as Shirley painted a lifestyle she was living completely fabricated for consumption by her mother.

Watching the two of them was like watching a couple of actors in a play. I didn't know the Shirley I was watching and certainly was seeing her mother for the first time with my own eyes and ears, and not through Shirley's.

Mother evidently approved of the way we were dressed, for when we arrived we knew she checked us out as if we were clients of hers, and when she smiled, oh, she smiled, but the smile never reached her eyes before it was gone. Of course, she would have approved of Shirley – she had selected and sent the dress and jewelry Shirley wore.

I noted two of us wore pearls. She called attention to hers by asking Shirley if she liked them while at the same time informing us they were baroque and a new gift. I waited for Shirley to ask, "from whom?" I knew Shirley well enough to know she couldn't care less, but I thought that remark was an opening for a discussion, and decided to keep my mouth shut. If she had someone else in her life, she would have to let Shirley know without my help.

Shirley didn't bite.

After the "dinner visit" ordeal, I dropped Shirley off at her apartment to change. She couldn't wait to hit a few bars.

I didn't see Shirley until Monday lunch, but then I didn't expect as much.

"How about twenty until payday?" she greeted a she sat down. I reached into my purse and handed over the ready folded twenty. This had become a routine – my loaning her a twenty every Monday until the end of the week.

We were all living from payday to payday, but from the time she and I met, she attached herself to me and I became her best friend and she one of mine. Somehow I also became her banker on Monday. Payday at the end of the week, she'd hand me a twenty. This went on and on until I didn't know whose twenty it was.

Then one day she asked for a twenty. I didn't have one on me and I didn't want to give her my emergency fifty hidden in my wallet. Since she was desperate and without funds, I asked my boss, who was in a nearby booth, if he had a twenty – he gave it to me – I gave it to her – then she gave it to me at the end of the week – I gave it to him, and then it started all over again. My boss accepted the twenty and dropped it in his desk drawer. Monday at noon, when I went into his office to tell him I was leaving for lunch, he took it out and handed it to me, and at lunch I handed the twenty to Shirley.

I never knew what my boss at that time, Marlon Brando Sr., thought about the twenty, he just went along handing me a twenty on Monday at noon. Perhaps he thought I was living beyond my means, but it was better than having to explain it was for my friend Shirley.

For Shirley was an alcoholic. She stopped by a bar after work each day for a drink or two....or three? But never missed a day of work. She drank all weekend, and never asked me for more than twenty on Monday.

Shirley and I didn't socialize after work. She went her way, I went mine. Her way was to stop at a bar. I never invited her to any of my parties. She never had any. But we did meet at different night clubs and parties often as we knew the same crowd and as usual Shirley, though she could hold her liquor, was always three sheets to the wind all weekend. When she'd see me, she made certain everyone else saw me too.

She'd make a loud announcement, "There's Al-lee! The purrr-fect laydee! She never gets in-tox-i-ca-ted! My mother even approves of her. La - dee - dah!"

Of course, people who didn't know either of us would expect a cat-fight, but those who did know us ignored it.

I always laughed and greeted her with, "And hello to you too." She was my friend Shirley. And drunk.

Monday at noon it was lunch and twenty. And always the desperate call.

"Ali, got to talk to you. My mother called."

This time it wasn't to meet more of Shirley's friends. She had approved of me and asked about me when she called Shirley, but didn't extend any invitations to dine with her and Shirley again.

Mother was coming to town once more. Shirley, as usual, had a problem whenever she did. This one was financial.

Fall turned into winter. Mother had sent Shirley a new collarless coat. She had previously given Shirley some sables. But Shirley's lifestyle didn't include a luxurious sables scarf, so, needing money, she had hocked the sables.

Now her mother had called to say she was coming to town and wanted to see the coat she had sent on Shirley when they dined, and suggested Shirley wear the sables since the coat had no collar. Shirley was in a panic, to put it mildly.

The suggestion was a command, as Shirley well knew. Shirley needed a couple hundred.

"Aleee! You have to bail me out!" Desperation filled her voice.

Ali to the rescue. Once more.

We got the sables out of hock, and as soon as her mother left town the sables went back into hock, and the money back into my bank account.

It was a long winter. I can't tell you the number of times we had to take those sables out of hock when her mother said she was coming to town, even if there were no definite plans to dine because she would be busy and would call if she could fit Shirley into her schedule. It stopped after her mother sent her a beautiful curry-colored high fashion wool coat with a real leopard shawl collar that extended halfway down her back. We had to give it to her – her mother really, really knew "fashion." Shirley never had to return anything she sent.

Everyone knew Shirley was around when we saw that stylish coat flung over a chair or on the floor. Wherever it landed when she shrugged it off.

Another Monday morning and another desperate "I must see you" phone call.

I sat waiting for Shirley at lunchtime when she blew in with a jolly "hello" to Lucy and a serious look on her face when she sat down. Then a hurried whisper, "I want you to keep a secret. You're the only one I'm telling. Promise you won't tell anyone."

"I promise. But if it's such a big secret, don't tell me," I declared.

"I want you to know, but no one else."

"Well...okay."

"I'm married."

My mouth must have popped open, for I closed my mouth because nothing came out of it. I was stunned speechless and just stared at her. Did I hear right? My friend Shirley is married! And she didn't want anyone else to know!

"I got married this weekend in Las Vegas," she continued ignoring my stupid, I'm sure, surprised look.

I finally found my voice. "I didn't know you were interested in anyone. You didn't tell me you were."

"I just met him Saturday."

"What!"

I was now more than surprised and my mouth flew open again. She continued surprising me with every word out of her mouth.

"He was in the Marines. It was love at first sight for him, and we flew to Las Vegas and got married."

"Where is he now?" I wanted to know.

"He's in my apartment. We're going to live in my apartment until he gets his stuff together. He just got out."

"Shirley," I reminded her, "your apartment is one tiny room with a pull-down wall bed, and a one-burner hot plate. It's too small for you and the clothes your mother sends, let alone closet space for a Marine."

How drunk was she? I wondered.

I also wondered what he thought of Mona Lisa. Shirley's only art was a large print of Mona Lisa that had a hole in it at the corner of her mouth. Shirley never remembered how it got there, but after a time the hole bothered her. She didn't want to part with Mona Lisa, so she lit up a cigarette, took a few puffs, extinguished it, and inserted it in the hole in the corner of Mona Lisa's mouth. As soon as you entered Shirley's studio apartment, the first thing that caught your eye was Mona Lisa smoking a cigarette. This told you a great deal about Shirley.

Our food arrived. We ate in silence for a moment. Then she very seriously revealed she didn't want to be like her mother living with a man over twenty years, but not marrying him though he wanted to marry her.

Now I knew why Shirley wanted her marriage a secret; she didn't want "mother" to learn of it. Shirley knew she would not approve of her marriage. I guess she'd have to sneak out to dine with "mother" when next she hit town.

So, my friend Shirley was married. I realized later she didn't tell me his name. Maybe she didn't remember it since she had been intoxicated when she changed names, and I didn't think to ask because I was in that surprised state.

Well, I kept her secret. Never met the Marine. We didn't talk about him. No one knew she was married. Did she still spend her time partying weekends? Who knew? I didn't. She was still asking for twenty on Mondays.

Months later on Friday, when she was returning the twenty, she announced, "I'm going to Santa Anita tomorrow and you're coming with us."

Us! She wanted me to go to the racetrack "with us!" Ah, ha! I was finally going to meet the Marine who we never spoke about. This would be interesting.

She didn't introduce me to him as her husband. Are we pretending they are not married?

Shirley had a Racing Form and she and I talked horses all the way on the long drive from Hollywood to the Santa Anita Racetrack. It was a good thing because I hadn't been following the horses and didn't know who was running, though I was aware of the names of a few jockeys. I decided I would put my money on whatever horse Bill Shoemaker was riding. Seemed like a safe bet to me as I hadn't been prepared for a day at the races, and didn't have that much money to lose.

Shoemaker was good to us that day; we all came home winners. That sounds like we won a bundle, but I only bet as much money as I could afford to lose and I know Shirley wasn't any richer, but Shirley's Marine had met a buddy, not by chance as it turned out, and he joined us. From their cheers and arm punching, the Marines did well enough to treat us to a prime rib dinner after the races. The big surprise of the day and night for me...my friend Shirley wasn't drinking!

What was that all about?

I couldn't wait for Monday's lunch, not only to confront her about the "blind date" she didn't tell me about. Monday couldn't come fast enough for me.

The first thing out of my mouth when Shirley dropped into the booth was, "You may have been drunk when you got married, but you sure picked a winner." Then confronted the "buddy" who she dismissed very conveniently.

"Oh, I forgot to tell you we were meeting him."

Forgot my foot. But he was a rugged Marine – a nice guy, with a great sense of humor, and it was easy to forgive her. Her Marine was also one of the nicest fellows who ever came down the pike. How lucky could she get? Evidently, she knew it because she said she wasn't drinking. She spent nights at home with him, and also weekends. He liked the ponies, so they had been going to the racetrack. Then she confided she was also spending a great deal of time working on a hush-hush system. A system?

It wasn't too long before I learned, only because she needed me, it was a system to win at the races.

"Ali, you've got to come to the races with me this Saturday," she insisted. "It takes two people to work the system."

That's when I discovered her Marine wasn't interested in a system, even if it was hers. He liked to pick his own winners, and losers.

After that, it was every Saturday at Santa Anita while Shirley tried to perfect her system. I had fun with my money and hers – and her Marine came through when she was wiped out. The Meet at Santa Anita closed and she closed down her system. I didn't understand what she was doing because she kept everything very close – God forbid someone stole her system before she perfected it. All I knew was she sat at a table with papers and forms and figures, and gave me money to bet Win, Place, or Show. I don't think she ever saw a race, she was so busy figuring God only knows what.

Her Marine would occasionally stroll by and tease with a remark out of the side of his mouth, "I hear the fix is in on the next race," and keep on walking, sending Shirley into a tizzy because I couldn't convince her he was pulling her leg.

As much as I enjoyed the races and the biggest winner picked-up-the-check dinners, I was glad the Meet was over and Shirley could get the "system" out of her system because she had been consumed by it. I was the only one she trusted to help her. As far as I could ascertain, it was going nowhere.

Little did I know Santa Anita Racetrack was the glue holding that marriage together, for Shirley was back on the party scene, alone – always stewed to the gills, not going home, sleeping wherever she found a bed or sofa. Someone always took care of her. Her Marine was constantly looking for her weekends. Everyone thought he was the latest boyfriend. He was still a secret.

It wasn't too long before the Marine could no longer take it, though he lasted much longer than I thought he would. They broke up for months, both miserable, and went back together for months. This was the routine for about a year. The split came when he finally realized and accepted she didn't want to, or couldn't, stop drinking. He tried, but felt he couldn't help her and decided he wouldn't watch her destroy herself and him in the bargain. She didn't think he'd leave her. Didn't he love her? Didn't he always come back? But he did leave.

Shirley stopped drinking hoping he'd return.

The months went by and he didn't return, nor did she hear from him. It may have shocked her into straightening out. She joined AA. She found some partners and played tennis nightly and on weekends. She went on a health kick too and was looking great. Her laughter could be heard again.

Shirley received a promotion at work. She accepted the Marine wasn't coming back – and she didn't seem depressed about it. I was glad she was taking the walkout so well and was the happy, carefree, funny Shirley again, who was also very happy with her promotion to a new job.

She called and cancelled luncheons because of her changed lunch schedule. Now we only had lunch on Monday for the twenty and Friday to return it. I missed her at lunch, and since we had often been joined by others, now I was the one looking to join a table or booth.

Then a very strange thing happened. Not to Shirley. To me. I received a phone call from one of the girls at the studio I had known a long time, but did not socialize. She was older than I, and married. She asked me to breakfast with her the following morning. I found it odd she suddenly wanted to breakfast with me after all these years we've known each other. Perhaps a male relative was coming to town and she needed to fix him up with a few dates was all I could think about. It had happened before with others, so I didn't think beyond that – just hoped whoever it was, was an okay guy as I didn't mind helping out a friend in need if I had nothing better to do.

When I arrived at the studio commissary she thoughtfully had my favorite breakfast, a heated bear claw and hot tea with lemon, already waiting. I thanked her profusely and dug right in. She didn't do the same as she only had coffee she held cradled in both her hands but didn't even bring to her lips for a sip.

"I don't know how to ask this of you, but I need a big favor," she threw out in a low voice, barely above a whisper.

There was something in her voice that made me stop eating, and I gazed at her wondering what was so serious.

She continued speaking. "Did you know your friend Shirley is having an affair with my husband?"

"Affair with my husband" seemed to bounce off the walls and smash into me.

I was glad I was sitting down or I would have fallen down. I had expected anything but that! Not with Shirley's history – her father and a female employee in his business, which caused the divorce in her family and made her a homeless drifter since childhood.

Bear claw forgotten, she now had my full attention. "I can't believe that," I gasped when I finally spoke.

"Believe it. She's working in the same office with him."

"Are you sure?" I persisted.

"Yes, I have photos of them," she said with a quiver in her voice. I thought she was going to cry.

"I've had them followed." Her voice cracked.

No wonder Shirley was so happy and couldn't make lunch.

"What do you want of me?" I inquired with dread.

"Everyone knows you're her best friend and always get her out of trouble. She only listens to you. I don't want my marriage to break up. Could you get her to stop seeing him? I don't know where else to turn."

I was numb by this time. My tongue was disengaged from my brain. I sat in silence.

"I don't want my husband to find out I know about them," I heard her whisper, overcome by emotions she was trying to control.

She was so distraught and uncomfortable talking to me about her husband, her feelings, and her marriage. I felt so very sorry.

For her.

For Shirley.

For her husband.

And for myself especially.

I didn't like having this marital problem dumped on me. But it had landed with a thump in my lap and I knew I'd have to confront it since she had convinced me she was very serious when she said:

"I would never, never let your friend Shirley break up my marriage."

This was the message I had to get across to Shirley without letting her know about our breakfast meeting.

I waited until Shirley and I were having lunch alone and dumped it in her lap. I stunned her when I said I heard she was involved with a married man. I was very careful not to tell her I received the news from his wife because I didn't want her running back to him with that information.

Shirley thought it was secret, but I let her believe it was all around town. That stunned her further. I even went so far as to reveal I heard she may be fired. Never revealing it was his wife who threatened it. That he was in solid, but she'd have to go. I felt more than sorry for Shirley – and myself in the middle of this entanglement. She didn't deny involvement, but said it wasn't as serious as I made it out to be. I didn't know if she was kidding me or herself. I only knew I wanted her out of this affair before his wife, in desperation, took matters further to end it, as it was very serious to her.

After our luncheon, I didn't hear from Shirley.

My guess. She was mad at the messenger. And, I wondered, how long.

It wasn't too long before I received a call from the wife who thanked me. Her husband was no longer "lunching" with Shirley nor was he "working" nights. And, no longer sleeping in the guest room, no longer came home late and didn't want to wake her. He was "back home."

She was "back in a happy marriage."

I didn't know if he was, and didn't ask.

But I did ask her not to be too happy to see me when next we met. I didn't want Shirley to put one and one together and get two. Shirley was one smart lady.

Although the wife was happy to have her husband back home, the call made me feel rather sad because I knew Shirley was probably hurting by another failed love. Yet, on the other hand, at the same time I felt relieved my friend Shirley was out of the triangle before it got ugly as it had been threatening to do, and she would lose a job she liked.

I heard Shirley was back on the bottle big time. We didn't lunch. She found a new crowd to hang with and new places to drink. I didn't see her socially anymore. I never was a drinking buddy. I didn't worry too much. I knew she'd come around sooner or later, and as usual we'd pick up as if nothing had happened and we had been seeing each other, and lunching all along.

Just as I was leaving for work one morning, as predicted, my friend Shirley did call.

"Could you pick me up and take me to work?"

"Car trouble?" I asked.

"Yeah. See ya."

When I picked her up I asked what the trouble was with her car. Was I in for a surprise!

"I was driving home after midnight Saturday night and had an accident."

"Are you injured?" I asked, concerned.

"No. I was too drunk to get hurt."

We both laughed, but I was curious. "What happened?"

"I left the local bar and was driving home and I had turned into my street. The next thing I knew there was glass flying, and fruit, and vegetables, and flowers, and I was sitting in my car in the middle of the produce department of the market on the corner."

I couldn't believe what I was hearing. We both laughed again as she continued to describe the broken plate glass window, the car covered in smashed produce. "It was a holy mess."

"What did you do? Call 911? The police?"

"No, I got out of the car, took the keys, and walked home and went to sleep."

"You did what?" This was incredulous.

"I went to sleep. The next morning I called the police and reported my car stolen. Later they called back and told me they found my car crashed in the market and were having it towed to a garage."

That was my friend Shirley, who was my friend in spite of her never-ending problems. That incident didn't slow her down.

Not many more weekends had passed before very early on the one morning I decided to sleep in, the shrill ringing of the phone woke me. I was tempted to roll over and ignore it, but it was too hard to do.

I picked up the phone and threatened, "This better be important."

"I need a lawyer."

She had my attention.

"Where are you?"

"Downtown in jail."

She hung up.

Hung up! I felt like screaming.

What had she done now to put her behind bars? I knew a few lawyers, but they were not criminal lawyers. They drew up movie contracts. I was now wide awake. Sleeping in was forgotten. Jail was serious in my mind. I needed someone to get my friend Shirley out of whatever trouble she was in with the law. I now had to wake a few friends to get the ball rolling. And being friends, they came through. But I felt I now owed them big time – not only for waking them before dawn.

After she was out of jail and we lunched, I heard her story as to how she wound up behind bars. As usual, it was Saturday night. She was on the way home and decided to stop by the local bar for one last drink. A very nice gentleman sitting near to her at the bar initiated a conversation. Naturally, he would. She was a most attractive, well-dressed girl. Then they shared a drink together. When the bartender blinked the lights the gentleman, who had learned Shirley lived in the neighborhood, asked her if she had anything at home. He didn't want to end the evening. She said she had a bottle of Jack Daniels and, with that said, they both left the bar together. As soon as they were out the door, they were joined by another gent and Shirley was informed she was under arrest.

When she asked, "What for?"

She was told, "For soliciting." And read her "her rights."

They were undercover cops.

She said sex was the last thing on her mind. She was just up for an all-night drinking party with a newfound drinking buddy.

Shirley learned from her lawyer why she was picked up. Her lawyer discovered there was a ring of "ladies of the evening" who had been picking up men late in the evening at the bars in and around the vicinity. The undercover cops were working on breaking up the ring.

"I don't want to tell you what else they said."

"Don't tell me there's more to this!"

"No. Nothing really," she hedged.

"Remember me? I'm the one who got you a lawyer, Shirley," I reminded her. "You can't not tell me."

What she hesitated telling me was her lawyer said the hooker would come into a bar just before closing time, sit at the bar next to or near a man, leave with him, and take him to a motel room – then leave with his money and valuables.

They said Shirley "came into the bar late in the evening and fit the description of a very attractive, well-dressed, high-class hooker."

I laughed till tears. "For goodness sake, Shirley, how were you dressed? What did you have on?"

"Oscar de la Renta. A new wild red outfit my mother just sent me. It was the first and last time I'll put that dress on!" She didn't appreciate my laughter. She didn't think being taken for a hooker was funny – not even a high-class one.

The lawyer got her out of this mess. She was so grateful, she made promises no one could keep. Notwithstanding, I accepted her gratitude never knowing what would be coming up next.

This episode kept her out of bars for some time. Then I learned she had moved out of that neighborhood and she was no longer working at the television station. No one had seen her around her usual haunts. Soon I discovered why. Beside the move out of her old neighborhood, she had a new boyfriend. But none of her old friends or mine had met or knew him.

Not too long afterwards on a Sunday morning my phone rang and didn't stop all day. Had I seen the papers? Shirley's boyfriend was found dead in her apartment! And she was taken in for questioning! We all went crazy. We were unable to get firsthand information.

Then we heard the death was reported a suicide, and we all came back to earth.

No one knew the whereabouts of Shirley. She had vanished. Everyone thought I should know, but I was in the dark. All were anxious about her – I wasn't the only one.

I had despaired of hearing from her, but couldn't believe she wouldn't call. The waiting was torture. Finally, it came.

She asked me to meet her at a place where we wouldn't be known or seen by anyone we knew. She was aware I would be worried about her. She waited until the questioning of her, her drinking buddies at the bar that night, and her neighbors, was over. She explained she didn't want to get me involved in any way with her or what had happened. She was protecting me, and that was the reason why she hadn't contacted me. Shirley was distraught, had deep feelings of guilt. We talked of her troubles and she related what happened that night.

She had met this guy at a bar. They began dating and soon he moved in with her. That particular night, they were out drinking and evidently had a violent disagreement in the bar. She told him she was through and he could no longer live with her; he had to move out. Shirley left the bar and he followed.

When they returned to the apartment, Shirley was hungry, so she went into the kitchen to fry a couple of eggs and make toast for herself – he stayed in the living room. The argument they had in the bar and on the way home continued and she repeated she was through with him – he had to get out – she was not kidding. He responded by threatening to kill himself.

Shirley said, "I laughed out loud in disbelief he would use killing himself to make me change my mind."

Then she heard a gunshot.

She rushed to the kitchen door, looked toward the sofa where he was lying, saw ceiling plaster falling down all around him and the floor. When she saw this, Shirley became angry he had done this and frightened her, and said, "I knew you didn't have the guts." Whereby, he put the gun to his head and blew out his brains while she looked on.

Neighbors had heard the first shot, and one had called 911 and reported it. The police arrived soon after the second shot and found a shocked, hysterical Shirley, along with a dead body, and eggs burning on the kitchen stove.

Shirley was taken into custody, questioned, and released hours later the next day after it was determined the wound was self-inflicted.

I did my best to console my friend Shirley. I couldn't believe what she had gone through, seeing him blow out his brains, and was still going through emotionally.

Shirley then disappeared again. No one had a glimpse of her. I worried because she was so depressed and had lost her love of life. She was not the Shirley I knew, happy-go-lucky, who wore a smile on her face and was always good for a laugh.

As usual, she called out of the blue and we got together. She filled me in on what had happened in her life since we had last seen each other.

It was heartbreaking to hear.

Shirley was unable to work. Her mother sent her money, but just enough to live on. She was also in therapy and AA. She had reached bottom.

After the suicide, Shirley was so utterly bereft and guilty, she felt compelled to end her own life.

She tried to make light of it as she confided about her attempt – turning all the stove gas burners and oven on in her apartment. Then she stretched out on the kitchen floor, waiting to die – only the neighbors smelled gas became frantic and called the Gas Company. They immediately dispatched an emergency crew who discovered the gas was coming from her apartment. After knocking and receiving no response, the landlady opened the door with her passkey – Shirley was found on the floor, revived, and hospitalized.

When she recovered, she was evicted from her apartment.

Remorseful, she still wanted to end her life, so she went to the hardware store and purchased a length of hose. Then drove and parked on a dirt road in the hills off Mulholland Drive overlooking the San Fernando Valley. She inserted the hose into the exhaust pipe and brought it around into the car.

Shirley sat with motor running – her eyes closed and waited to die. Instead, she heard a knocking on the opposite side window. She turned at the sound, opening her eyes, and stared into the face of a policeman who was patrolling the area and saw her parked automobile. He gave her a stern warning about how dangerous it was for a girl to sit alone in the car viewing the valley.

The policeman then walked away, got back into his cruiser, and waited for her to move. Shirley discarded the hose out her door and followed him as he drove up the rutty dirt road. She checked in the rearview mirror and saw that the hose had become dislodged from the exhaust pipe by the bumpy road and had fallen away.

Despite the failures, Shirley was still filled with remorse and determination.

In her next attempt to end her life, she explained, she cut her wrists and fainted from the sight and loss of the blood. She was found by a friend who saw her car in front of her apartment. He decided she must be home and when she didn't answer his knocks and banging on her door, he broke in, and she was rescued by his 911 call for paramedics.

By the time she finally got around to calling me, her wrists had healed and she was wearing wide matching silver bracelets hiding the still-red scars.

After all this trauma, Shirley decided she was unable to kill herself, so she returned to therapy, which her mother again paid for, and again went back to AA meetings. She was now trying to put her life back together instead of trying to end it.

She acknowledged she knew I was there for her, but felt so embarrassed by all that had happened – and with her life spiraling out of control, that she couldn't bring herself to see me until she went back to therapy.

On departing, I wished her well, and I left her with a "you have my number," and her promise to keep in touch.

After a time, I lost contact again, but I felt confident I would be hearing from her eventually. I just prayed the therapy and AA was helping.

It was many months later I had news of her – Shirley had a new boyfriend and was madly in love, but the relationship was strained – she evidently was more in love than he was – he would see her for a while, and then drop her.

I didn't like what I heard. I felt she was still very fragile – too emotionally fragile to be in this type of relationship.

I thought she was still in therapy, but she again had stopped. Her mother had given up on her since she stopped her therapy sessions.

Then I heard she had no money. She couldn't get an apartment – she would stay with her boyfriend for a few days, and then he would put her out when he met someone else he desired. He was a well-known player.

It went on this way until he found a girl he cared for, and he moved her in with him.

When Shirley came around, he told her to "get lost." But she wouldn't stay lost. She was obsessed with him and came by every night – sitting on his doorstep. His current girlfriend was being harassed by Shirley, as was he...so they moved.

Shirley became a stalker.

She followed him until she discovered where he had moved. She left notes in his mailbox. On his door. On his automobile. He called the police and Shirley was given a harassment and stalking warning. Everyone heard about what she was doing from him, no one saw her. She had no phone, nor apartment. The word was she was living in her car.

I wanted to cry.

It saddened me to hear she was in such mental, emotional, and financial straits. I tried desperately to find her. But failed. I didn't know where she could be. The word was out I was looking for her.

And I waited for her call.

Then the call I never wanted came.

My friend Shirley had been found dead in the trunk of her car at a park across from the apartment building of the man she loved and who had rejected her.

She had been dead for a few days.

I was crushed.

Days went by and I found I still waited. I couldn't help myself from believing she would call. That we would have lunch, and she would ask for twenty.

I received another disturbing call soon afterwards. Her very wealthy father had died. He remembered her in his will and his lawyers had been looking for Shirley for months, but had been unable to find her until news of her death was reported in the newspaper. Her father had left her very wealthy. He had set up a trust fund for her.

My friend Shirley who was destitute, living in her car, died an heiress.

A year later.

A small package, brown paper wrapped, with no name nor return address was delivered to me. It had been mailed from northern California.

Inside was a designer scarf and a handwritten unsigned few words:

I think Shirley would like you to have this.

I recognized her favorite designer scarf. The one she most often wore. I could only assume it came from "you know who."

That was when I finally knew she would never call me again. And, I put "My Friend Shirley" to rest.

Around Our Dinner Table

Las Vegas is so close it was, and is, a weekend getaway. I don't know anyone who hasn't been to Las Vegas for a weekend. One of my sisters, Mary Christmas, lived in Las Vegas, so we were lucky we didn't have to pay the high prices for a hotel room, we could spend our money on "seeing the star entertainers", and spend quarters trying to hit the jackpot.

There are "promotions" that are taken advantage of during the year. But these are not always available when you are available. That was so at this particular time, but this lucky couple did luck out when they discovered the Dunes was closing.

Las Vegas Honeymoon Star

Tired after the wedding celebration, then driving almost three hundred miles to Las Vegas, we were happy to finally reach the Dunes Hotel where we were to spend our honeymoon. We felt so lucky to get the reservation. Even though we were both employed, a Vegas honeymoon in a hotel, not a motel, was not in our budget.

But, as luck would have it, we discovered the Dunes on the Vegas Strip was closing and rooms were available at motel prices.

We had learned dining and entertainment had been discontinued – and the casino closed. This suited us fine as we did not come for gambling. We just wanted to see a few shows and spend time at poolside getting a Vegas tan. Though we were disappointed there would be no breakfast in bed, we didn't mind "No Dining" because we had planned on dining at some of the new hotels.

Also, we were more interested in seeing the headliners who were in town – top entertainer Frank Sinatra headed the list that lit up the Vegas Strip. We knew if you played one of the big hotels you were a star! We were anxiously looking forward to seeing a few of the biggest and brightest.

So upon arrival we checked in at the Dunes on the Vegas Strip – Mr. and Mrs. Todd Thompson. Our room was in every sense of the word a honeymoon suite with a sweeping view of the desert sands vanishing in the distance. We were beyond pleased with the plush king-size bed and bathroom with an unreal shower – it was so immense.

We refreshed, and before departing the hotel for our night on the town, we decided to prowl the premises one last time since it was being demolished. We strolled through the empty, silent, gambling casino – gaming tables covered in ghostly white awaiting movers, and then on to the dining room with stacked tables and chairs, and crossed the lobby to the Cocktail Lounge. All that was left of the glamour and glitter of Las Vegas nights was a shimmering silver curtain and an ebony grand piano and bench on the barren stage located behind the bar. Suddenly, I saw my husband stroll across the stage, sit on the piano bench, and finger the keys. So, I trailed and leaned on the piano.

He looked up at me. "This is for you, Martha," he said softly.

Todd played our song – the one we had danced to just hours before. The music filled the lounge, for he played beautifully, and when he finished just as I leaned to give him a "thank you" kiss, I was startled midway because, unbeknownst to us, we had an audience.

A gentleman clapped and yelled, "Encore! Encore!"

I gave Todd the interrupted kiss, then joined in the clapping. "Todd, you're a star! Take a bow," I urged.

Ever the gentleman, he bowed to his audience with a flourish.

I looked on, enjoying the moment: Todd entertaining and taking a bow on the Lounge stage, and locked it away with the other memories of our wedding day.

Todd and I came to Las Vegas to see a few star performances and made history, for my husband was the last star to play the Dunes on the Las Vegas Strip!

Clean Out the Refrigerator Casserole

I overslept and arose later than usual, so here I am, rushing around because when I opened the dishwasher to put in my breakfast dishes I had to unload and put away last night's dishes. I know, I should have done it last night, but I confess, I was watching television too late and now I was rushing around. You see, I now have this routine that is guided by the Food Channel. I'm addicted to this particular spiked-hair chef with great charisma who has become a celebrity, along with being a good cook, and he's on late at night. My day ends with him.

I'm a retired, at an early age, chef. Actually, I didn't retire, my father retired me. Because it was the nineties, and since I was a child of the nineties, you know why my father retired me. And now, perhaps, you can understand my interest in food.

We owned two restaurants. That is, Dominick did. Dominick, that's my father, or Dom as everyone, including me, called him, was chef of one, and I the other before he sold it out from under me.

Now, I'm again unemployed, and in need of a roof over my head, and felt I couldn't continue shuttling from friend to friend's living room sofas, so I headed where? The place I went when I had no place else to go. Just like everyone I knew in the same predicament. Home.

I returned to the family nest. The very same where I couldn't wait to grow up so I could leave. My folks now had a guest room – formerly my room where I spent my boyhood.

It wasn't too long before I heard whispers, well not whispers as my mother had to speak loudly for my father was hard of hearing and in denial, therefore he didn't have a hearing aid. There was nothing wrong with my hearing, and I was no dummy.

It didn't take me long to know I'd have to be moving on after I overheard, "Is he still sleeping? When is he going to get a job? How long is he going to camp out here?"

I had no money to speak of. I had friends who were all tapped out too. Some in worse shape than I. I knew I was mooching off my parents. I didn't like it. In fact, I hated that I was. But I was beaten down by the time of my life. Where had I gone wrong? When I asked myself where I was and where I was going, I just rolled over and escaped into the arms of Morpheus.

And then one day I awakened disoriented, that is until I heard loud voices traveling down the hall stealing through my partially open door. Dom said he desperately needed help at the restaurant, and my mother's loud voice responded:

"Don't look at me!"

This propelled me out of bed into the shower. How quickly my problem was solved. I would volunteer to help Dom out of his predicament and be the shining white knight. Worries about where I would drop my clothes and lay my head ran down the drain along with the cold water running off my body.

I made myself scarce until Dom left for the restaurant, then I sauntered out to the patio, had a cup of coffee with my mother, and left for the day without giving away my plans. Actually, I didn't say where I was going because I didn't know if Dom would welcome me into the family fold, yet again.

I stopped by to kill some time with a friend, and left when I knew the lunch bunch would be crowding into the restaurant. I came with them. Without asking Dom if he wanted a hand, seeing the need, I came to the rescue. I pitched right in making meatballs or sausage on sourdough, filling soup bowls with Dom's specialty minestrone, and cups with hot coffee. Dom acknowledged me by giving me orders to fill. And by the end of the day, I was back in the fold.

The next few days I brought in a couple old hands who had bused for me and needed work. Dom let me know he wanted to "spruce up the place," so I called an artist friend, who always could use "paint money" to design a mural for one of the walls. Also, rounded up a few more always-low-on-funds buddies to paint the other walls. For free meals. I was racking up goodwill all over the place without even trying. Especially so with Dom.

After several weeks of free room and board, along with laundry and the use of my mother's credit card for gas, I wasn't rolling in dough, but I had more than a few bucks in my billfold. Not enough to take a run up to Frisco or Vegas for a weekend, but at least I could stand for a couple of beers, and I could go back to really tarring up my lungs. My mother didn't understand why I started smoking again. What she really didn't understand, I had never stopped smoking. I just stopped buying cigarettes because I found I'd rather buy a burger and fries. Let's face it, my friends had lit up two when I was around.

After the exhilaration of lifting myself up off the floor, so to speak, I was now looking for an escape from the restaurant. It wasn't that I didn't like working there, but I was working for my father, in his restaurant, not mine. Things were done his way. I was used to being top dog, making decisions, and when my mother began asking when I was going to get an apartment now I was employed, that's when I discovered they didn't realize I was a temp at the restaurant. I seriously started to look for a way out.

I couldn't understand though why she was pushing me out. I was her son, for goodness sake. I had been raised in this house. I thought of it as my home. But, it's amazing, once I left, I would stop by, and I didn't till now realize, I was a visitor. It had been my room all my life – no one could go into it. Now I could no longer claim it. It wasn't my room. It was the guest room. It wasn't my house. My home. It was my parents'.

It saddened me I was a guest with no place to call home, and they had cut the cord – but I hadn't. I couldn't even let myself think of when that happened.

Things were going well at the restaurant. Dom was very pleased with the friends I had brought in. Business was humming along. We were rushed during breakfast, coffee breaks, and lunch, which I liked, but enjoyed slow times too. Dom, as I said, was happy with my friends and the "spruced up place." Then my mother dropped a bomb. Dom had received a very lucrative offer for the "spruced up" restaurant. She urged him to take it. It was time for him to retire so they could travel while they were still young enough and healthy enough. She felt they owed it to themselves.

I went into shock. But not numb enough not to ask her when he was going to tell me. After he sold it? I discovered he planned to tell me at work that day. He had been mulling it over for a few days before telling my mother, now she urged me to lean on him to sell. It wouldn't be the first time she'd ask me to conspire with her when she wanted something, but this time was different. And though I had been thinking of moving on, I wasn't ready. I liked to have someplace to land whenever I bailed out.

When I did get to the restaurant, it wasn't long before Dom took a break with me and disclosed his decision to sell the place. I didn't have to "lean on him," his mind was made up. He didn't even notice I wasn't surprised. I guess he knew my mother well enough to know she'd tell me.

Dom moved fast after he decided to take the offer, and it wasn't long before I was again not only looking for a place I wanted to work, but also a place to park the body.

A friend had recently divorced and he decided to let out a few rooms to pay for lawyering and alimony. And let's face it, he didn't like rattling around in the big house alone with memories confronting him every time he walked in the door.

I was his first tenant. A few more friends filled the other beds. It was amazing how fast word got around, and before long it began to look like a frat house. Trying to help our friend get over the breakup of his marriage soon began taking its toll on all of us. We decided to end the all night partying and just have a few friends in for dinner and watching sports on the giant screen in the home theater.

Since I had been a chef, it was only natural I was the designated cook. The kitchen was my domain. Everyone seemed to gather there – when we weren't going through a few six packs, watching Kobe Bryant and the Lakers running miles back and forth across the court hardwood floor dunking baskets.

Since I was without gainful employment, while the others were at work, I was planning meals and grocery shopping. It wasn't long before I was glued to the kitchen TV, watching the daytime cooking shows for inspiration. The refrigerator reflected this, as there was a mélange of leftovers – Italian, Mexican, Chinese, Southern – sausage, meatballs, pork and beef roast, chicken, rice and noodles fighting for space on the shelves. It dawned on me nobody was eating leftovers.

Why don't people like leftovers? I wondered. Of course, the working stiffs couldn't face leftovers early in the morning. They didn't even have a cup of coffee before leaving, preferring to stop by Starbucks. I didn't blame them, I had always done the same. But to get back to the leftovers, I confess I like spaghetti for breakfast. I reason the base is dough, just like toast base is dough. Oh, well, I couldn't possibly eat all the leftovers for breakfast and lunch, dough or no dough. My conscience wouldn't allow me to feed the garbage disposal. You see, I was indoctrinated from an early age to think of the poor starving people of the world. Even though I didn't, at the time, comprehend starving, the thought of masses of starving people all over the world still comes forth from the depths of my being where it lies, waiting to pounce, therefore all the leftovers.

So, here I am, standing with the refrigerator door wide open, gazing at a few dinner leftovers while I contemplated a menu. A couple of the guys had dropped the news their current girlfriends were invited to dinner and a movie. That's why I had opened the refrigerator – to find out if salad greens and fresh vegetables should be added to my grocery list.

As I'm gazing, and thinking, and letting all the cold air out of the refrigerator, I had a brainstorm.

One of the food shows, I don't remember which, featured a casserole the cook had made from a leftover pork roast. This inspired me. I began pulling out the leftover meats. There was the beef roast, only enough for a man-size sandwich, a piece of pork, a sausage, and the ravaged carcass of a spit roasted chicken. There was not enough of anything for the recipe I recalled. But on looking further, I discovered leftover Chinese vegetables from our Chinese takeout, and likewise from our Italian takeout – a goldmine, fettuccine noodles with mushrooms. After all this was out of the refrigerator, I saw shining, two foil wrapped packages that yielded a bonanza, a couple of carrots and carrots and peas.

By this time I was intrigued by the array of food before me, and my years in a restaurant, plus the daily dose of the Food Channel where I talked back to the chefs, made me think with help from what I could find on the pantry shelves, I could conjure a casserole for the evening meal. It now became a challenge, and I set about my task. The one thing I knew for certain, it had to be in a cream sauce. No tomato sauce.

The dinner was a resounding success, if I say so, myself. Everyone was nicely fortified from the bar by the time they came to the table. The girlfriends, I noticed, were not dainty, push-food-around-the-plate eaters. Everyone put away the casserole with gusto. They all had seconds, and when one girlfriend was leaving, she asked for the bit left for her roomie who was "into cooking." I was more than happy to send it on the way with her.

The next morning I received a call from her requesting the recipe. Her roomie was intrigued by the delicious surprise with every bite, and she wanted to make the casserole for her boyfriend.

Soon afterward one of the guys called from work. He had told his colleagues about the movie and great casserole, and every girl at the firm wanted my casserole recipe. It seems all the girls were looking for a way to a man's heart.

Don't you hate it when you eat something delicious and want to eat it again, and yet again, and the host or hostess refuses to give you the recipe, or worst still one will be happy to give you the recipe, but then leave out the most important ingredient that made you ask for her recipe in the first place? I didn't want to be like either of them.

I was in a quandary. How could I confess I had cleaned out the refrigerator and gave the edible mess to my drunken friends? I had to do better than that. I had to come up with a casserole recipe. But it had to be something no one had ever tasted before.

Buoyed by the knowledge everyone loved casseroles, by the end of the day I was hustling to make another casserole with a cream sauce, hoping they'd forget the previous casserole and I could then pass on a recipe.

I came up with a vegetable lasagna in a cream sauce with a whisper of nutmeg. I had decided I needed some meat. I didn't have but a couple of sausages I had overlooked, so I took them out of the casing, crumbled them and scattered them over the top. This casserole, too, was delicious with the delicate white sauce and vegetables, but when you hit the too hot spicy sausage, in my opinion, it went downhill. Fortunately, there wasn't very much sausage and the next forkfuls soothed the palate, but did not make my original casserole forgotten.

After a few attempts to make everyone forget my original casserole, I finally had to confess I didn't have a recipe, it was just something I threw together with what I had on hand. It didn't wash; no one believed me.

Now everyone who had been at the dinner was having discussions about the ingredients in the casserole. One remembered a whisper of ginger, another peapods and said it was a Chinese casserole, another pork, and yet another roasted chicken, and argued about a pork and chicken casserole.

The never forgotten casserole had taken on a life of its own, for whenever food was mentioned within the group, it was brought up and discussed ad nauseam.

By this time, I had it with casseroles. I had made a big mistake making them because the comparisons were never ending. The original was not forgotten, and I was sick and tired of being hounded for the recipe, for by now it developed that everyone we had ever met or knew yearned for this mysterious out-of-this-world casserole recipe. No one remembered they had been drunk when they ate it, and didn't know what they were eating. Therefore, I decided to take a vacation from cooking and informed everyone at the house, it was either order in pizza, Kentucky Fried Chicken, Chinese, Carl's Burgers and Fries for dinner, or they could eat out.

In the meantime, since I didn't have to grocery shop when not out and about, I still turned to the Food Channel, and also flicked through magazines arriving for my friend's ex-wife. His lady had subscribed to every magazine in print. That was when, one morning, I saw a full page ad announcing a contest with a $50,000 First Prize for a new recipe using the cream sauce from the company sponsoring the contest. I glanced at it and resumed turning the pages.

Days passed, but that $50,000 prize came to mind at odd times. The more it did, the more the thought of entering the contest crossed my mind. And the more I kept pushing it aside, the more it haunted me. It wasn't long before I again picked up the magazine and, this time, read the rules. I qualified!

Now I racked my brain for a new recipe using a cream sauce, and watched, day and night, all the shows on the Food Channel for something I could improve on. I never realized there were so many ways hamburger could be used or garnished. But it didn't do me any good. In my mind, lowly hamburger didn't marry cream sauce and win a prize. But parked away back in the recess of my brain, there was the niggling thought; I knew the perfect blend, but I wouldn't let it escape. And abandoned the search for a winning recipe using a cream sauce.

Then, unwittingly one day, the $50,000 Prize loomed large and overcame any reluctance I had. It burst forth, sending me hurrying to my laptop. I wrote down a recipe for "Michael's Clean out the Refrigerator Casserole," put on my running shoes, and with envelope in hand, dashed off to the nearest post office.

Around Our Dinner Table

I was taking Christopher and Marisha, when young children, for a walk one day when child-sitting and we came upon an apartment garage sale. They both rushed for the toys, as if they didn't have enough at the house, and I joined them, walking through everything you could imagine laid out on the grass, and a colorful bowl caught my eye. I picked it up and examined it for chips and cracks. There was none, and the sticker price on the bottom was five dollars. The young lady who saw me examining it said her aunt had given it to her. I bought it along with the toys the children wanted, came home, and put it in the garage where I have storage cabinets, because I really didn't have any place for it at the time.

Then one day, years later, I thought about it after I had seen one similar for over a hundred dollars. I got out the bowl, took the five dollar price sticker off the bottom and discovered "Made in Italy" and a name – same as the one for over a hundred.

Instead of feeling "lucky", I began to feel bad because they were college kids who were having the garage sale and they probably didn't know the value of the bowl. I wished I could take it back. Never thinking it would inspire me years later.

Garage Sale

Hi! Trixie, on your way home from work, stop by and I'll buy you a drink...if you don't have a hot date, I'll even feed you. I have something interesting I want you to look at.

Body parts?

I'm going to assume you haven't a dirty mind and you mean auto – I won't keep you guessing – it's something you love – garage sale!

Start cooking!

I couldn't sleep. I just tossed and turned all night. Every night. For days.

Since Trixie, who is an arts major graduate and now works in a museum, had told me when she stopped by after work – and I fed her – the chair I had, really was an Eames and the small rug was Navajo – I've been bothered about them. They are parked in the corner of the living room. I didn't need them. They didn't fit anywhere. I don't even know why I bought them except the sweet, little gray-haired lady had been so nice, passing me a plate of cookies, urging I try them:

"These aren't store bought, dearie," and pouring me a paper cup of tart lemonade made with "lemons I picked this morning from my own tree in my back garden." Before I knew it, they were in my car.

I don't know why I'm such an easy mark. Sometimes kindness just makes me melt.

Just a few weeks ago, I had been driving home on a bright California Saturday morning from a Pilate's workout, and turned down a street I never took. The posted twenty-five miles per hour slowed me down, and that was when I came to the bright red signs GARAGE SALE and drove by driveways filled with someone's "let's get rid of this" junk. Evidently, everyone in this lovely neighborhood was cleaning out their garages in a community garage sale.

Why I stopped I'll never know. I NEVER stop at garage sales – I have enough of my own junk I should put out on my driveway with a "giving away" sign.

Now you know why I have a chair and rug stuck in a corner of my living room and because of it, I can't sleep – I'm feeling so very guilty about them. Why did I text Trixie? Why did we toast the "garage sale finds" and the money I would get from auctioning them off? All that money no longer danced around in my brain – all I could think of was the very nice, little old lady who was so glad to get rid of them she would have paid me to take them away if I was a "garage sale junkie" and knew how to barter. Her grandson had left them "stored" in her garage when "he went off to college years ago," and "he probably didn't know they even existed anymore."

More information than I needed, but it just added to my guilt as my imagination saw this poor guy stuck with college loans, needing money more than I did.

Sunday morning, I rolled out of bed, feeling sleep deprived after I had tossed and turned another night, and took a quick shower. As I crossed the living room to the kitchen to make breakfast, and glanced at the corner – I came to a firm decision. Stop with the guilt trip. The chair and rug had to go! Money be damned, they were ruining my life. Forget breakfast! I loaded them into my car and sped off.

When I drove up and took out my "finds" at the garage sale house, I saw a vintage Lincoln convertible parked in the driveway and a sandy-haired man in khaki cargo pants and white t-shirt walking around the car – he had just opened the door and was about to get in.

I rushed to the driveway as fast as I could, lugging the chair and rug, loudly shouting, "HEL-LOW there!"

He turned....and stared, taking me in – then slammed the door shut as I hastened up the drive. The look that came my way stopped me cold in my tracks as he came toward me asking:

"Is that MY chair and rug?"

I wanted to drop them and run. Instead, I put them down and faced his blue eyes shooting sparks.

"I bought them at the garage sale a few Saturday's ago," I explained, which didn't change his attitude towards me. He still stood and stared. I thought, *he knows it's an Eames chair and Navajo rug.*

"Can we talk?" I ventured with a smile.

"Make it fast...I'm hungry." Smile didn't work. He was still staring at me as if I stole the chair and rug from the nice, little old lady.

Well, maybe he thought I did if they belonged to him, and he knew their value. I felt I had to defuse this time bomb.

Hurriedly, I rattled off, "I bought the chair and rug at the garage sale a few weeks ago and when I got home with them, my girlfriend, Trixie – who is an art major graduate – she works in a museum – immediately recognized the Eames chair and the Navajo rug – she told me they were valuable, and we were so excited because of my good luck find – now I'm bringing them back because I couldn't sleep – I didn't know if the nice, little old lady I bought them from knew how much they were worth…" I was babbling, because he was standing there, twirling his sunglasses, never taking his sky blue piercing eyes off me before interrupting.

"That nice, little old lady is my grandmother, and she and I just went a few rounds because she decided to get rid of all my "junk" stored in her garage. You didn't, by any chance, buy a football too?"

My back was up now. He was making me feel guilty for buying them from that nice, little old lady, who happened to be his grandmother.

"What would I want with a football?" I answered indignantly.

"What would you want with *my* chair and rug?" he retorted.

So...he was annoyed because she got rid of his football too. "Are you a football player?" He looked like he could be a quarterback.

"No, but I was a quarterback in high school – and THAT was a winning game football."

"Well, I don't have it, so chalk one up for me!"

Was he still taking his loss to his grandmother by going a few rounds with me? In your dreams. I noticed he didn't have on a wedding ring – who'd have him? Good looks or no good looks, what a grump!

"Here's *your* chair and rug!" I pushed them further toward him in the middle of the driveway, and as I turned to go, I tossed off over my bare shoulder, "Nice meeting you!"

"Hey. WAIT! How much did you pay for these?"

I stopped and turned at his question. "Forget it!" I wanted to get away.

He smiled. It seemed he enjoyed having riled me. But it was too late to exchange smiles and civil conversation, as far as I was concerned.

"You paid for these, didn't you? Then by law they now belong to you," he said, in a friendly manner.

"Owe me!" I snapped, and again turned to go, even though his sky blue eyes were getting to me and he was being pleasant.

"I'm hungry. I'm on my way to get something to eat. Come on, get in," he ordered. "I'll buy you brunch and we'll talk and settle this."

"You're talking about a settlement? Are you a lawyer?" I questioned as I halted and faced him.

"How did you guess?" He clicked opened the garage door, picked up the chair and rug, put them in the garage, came back, and I was strapped in his car before I could even think of what I had been taught as a child – "NEVER GET INTO A CAR WITH A STRANGER." One triumphant with smiling blue eyes. I might now add.

I didn't think he would accept the price I thought about putting on my "garage sale lucky finds" when we negotiated over coffee – which by the way, I wasn't going to make until I consulted Trixie. This very high priced lawyer made a big mistake when he gave me "free advice" by telling me in the driveway since I paid for the chair and rug, they were mine.

There followed days of negotiating lunches and dinners where he did his utmost to charm me into making me like him. Make that love him. But I was onto his game. I kept raising the ante, thinking over and weighing everything in our negotiations – while he did all the right things, making me fall head over heels. But I never let him know I was drowning in his blue eyes while raising the ante and leading him on. Down the aisle.

All these great lunches and dinners – he really knew the most interesting romantic places that always had the best food too – wasn't too hard to take.

After all the romantic wining and dining, this irresistible charmer then wanted me to take a day trip out of the country with him. He had to go to Mexico for a client on business for "just a day" whose private company plane he said was at his disposal. I made him convince me to go with him to Mexico, if we could still have time to negotiate. Once there, he then decided we stay overnight. I reluctantly agreed. Wink! Wink!

Because he had been busy most of the day for his client, I shopped, and one of my "lucky finds" was a Mexican wedding dress, which I promptly decided to wear that evening to dinner. Hint! Hint! When I woke up next morning with a tequila hangover, I was married. Surprise! Surprise!

A few days later, I was helping Kenneth hang my garage sale find Navajo rug on the wall with the Eames chair directly below it in his luxurious law office.

"I haven't lost a case yet!" Ken said, congratulating himself as he stood back and looked at them, grinning. He heard Barbara snicker, and wondered what she would say if he told her he wanted them in his office to remind him how greatly he had enjoyed his summer vacation letting Barbara twist him around her little finger until she "caught" him.

"What was that about?" he asked instead.

"Haven't lost a case yet? Ha! Ha!" I said grinning too, rolling my eyes, thinking oh, what a delight this wonderful blue-eyed brilliant but naive lawyer was! I wondered what he would say if I told him my garage sale find hanging on his wall was one of the best deals I ever made when we negotiated over some tequila in Mexico, and that I went on the trip prepared to raise the ante, that included a marriage license and wedding ring!

"I'm glad you decided to hang the Navajo rug here," she said instead.

What Barbara didn't know – when I saw her rushing toward me that Sunday morning, I felt like I had been kicked in the gut by a mule, and feigned anger to hide it, as well as my surprise at seeing her rushing toward me. I couldn't give a tinker's damn about my chair and rug – or my football!

I had just gone a few rounds with my dear, sweet grandmother who I let convince me "they went to the loveliest girl I had ever met." And there she was – hauling *my* things up the driveway and laying them at my feet. My tall, blonde dream girl was in my grandmother's driveway in Bermuda shorts and a halter top, babbling away about a garage sale I couldn't give two figs about while I gazed at her in a daze staring, trying to figure out how to maneuver "this dream girl" into my car...and my arms.

Oh yes, I was the client with business in Mexico – that business was to make wedding arrangements and keep the tequila flowing, and when the time came, to remember which pocket held the wedding ring engraved "Ken loves Babs" I'd been carrying around for weeks.

Maybe I should tell her.

"I'm hungry…buy you lunch," he said instead ushering her out the door.

Someday....Maybe.

Memories of Spring and the Crack of the Bat

Ah, spring was at long last here after a harsh winter. The windows were wide open to the breeze blowing the lace curtains, and for us children it was a time to play outdoors. I could hear my young brothers, Michael and John, in the attic where they were making a racket enthusiastically searching for their bats, mitts, and baseballs. I could never understand then how throwing a ball back and forth to each other was any fun. But it seemed whenever we were sent out to play in the yard, they'd grab their mitts on the run, hit the yard, and start throwing that hard ball back and forth, back and forth while we played tag or hide and seek. On Saturdays, a few friends with gloves would gather, and then they'd leave for the field nearby. Before long, they were joined by others and they were hitting the ball and running around yelling for hours. My mother always knew where my brothers were when she saw the missing gloves.

My brothers grew into their teens, but it was only Michael, when spring sprung forth, who had a leather mitt dangling from hand or under his armpit, and a baseball stretching the left side pocket in his jacket or pants when he left the house. Looking for someone else with a glove, I don't doubt.

I didn't pay any attention to my brother's yackety-yak, actually they didn't want any girls hanging out with them and we'd be chased away if we entered their space. Consequently, I wasn't in on their baseball chatter, and therefore was unaware there were baseball leagues – big, minor, or sandlot. Of course, I wasn't supposed to, I was a girl as I was constantly reminded when I wanted to join in any of their games, like caddie.

I knew there were ballplayers because my brothers had baseball cards they were flipping, and I also saw those flipping cards with other boys their age. I just didn't understand how they could get much fun out of doing that. Little did I know they were flipping for player cards they didn't have and coveted. Then they spent hours at night talking about these cards. Once I listened thinking I could learn what was so interesting about the cards, instead I overheard them talking about stealing! Stealing what sounded like bases! But didn't let on I heard them before they chased me away. Although I didn't learn anything about the cards by eavesdropping, I was overjoyed by what I had heard because "stealing" was information I could use as a bargaining chip when wheeling and dealing with them. You needed all the arrows in your quiver you could get when living with boys. My brothers exchanged cards if they had two or whatever, and heaven help us if one of us sisters dared to ever touch them. So, I couldn't tell you what they were all about because I thought it was dumb and wasn't interested enough after that one time trying to discover what was so engaging.

Until later…

My brother Michael was about fifteen, which made me about ten or eleven years old. Our family went to church each Sunday en masse. Then came home and sat down to a formal Sunday dinner. Afterwards, we children went out to play with friends having been admonished not to get dirty. My two brothers, since they were older, would disappear, ignoring the edict "stay around where I can see you." Where they went I didn't know nor did I care. But Sundays at our house, when we weren't going to my Uncle Charlie's farm, or on a picnic, or visiting my grandmother, was a day of quiet relaxation and for children being "good." That meant "no fighting," which usually consisted of name calling, or pushing and shoving, or pulling hair, and one of us running to my mother, crying.

But this particular Sunday turned out to be different for me, for I was exposed to a sports world I didn't know existed that changed the way I saw my two brothers. I never looked at them as one of us children again, for they were living in a grown-up world outside the family where strangers knew and claimed them as their own.

My younger sisters played in the back garden and I sat on the front porch top step, blissfully dreaming of travelling to far off places, which I usually did when I had alone time as a child.

It wasn't long before I became aware a great number of men and boys had hurried by, going down toward Main Street. Curiosity got the better of me and I cried out, "Where is everyone going?"

"Your brother's pitching!" a man called back.

Pitching? Pitching horseshoes was all I knew. Nevertheless, it brought me instantly to my feet, for I had suddenly decided I would join the parade going down the street. Without bothering to tell anyone I was leaving, I left the porch steps to find out what was happening with horseshoes since it involved one of my brothers.

I have to say here I kept my eyes and ears open because I was the eldest girl in the family and had to have the answer to my mother when she'd ask where my little sisters, and even my elder brothers, were at any given moment, and what they were doing. Since I was her eyes and ears, I was always alert to what was going on with everyone. I had never heard anything about my brothers' involvement in horseshoes. True, I observed them pitching horseshoes when all the boys got together, but my brothers never were any better or worse than the other kids they played with. Since I had my hand on the pulse of what was going on in the neighborhood gang, is it any wonder I was so curious?

On the way down the block as I scurried to Main Street across the highway to the farmer's field, I learned my eldest brother, Michael, was a baseball player. That my brother was a pitcher. The best. That my brother had pitched a no-hitter, said with awe, the Sunday before. That my brother was pitching again today, and everyone wanted to see my brother Michael pitch.

This was unexpected stunning information and though it left me bewildered, I came to the conclusion there was a ball game of sorts that my brother Michael played in which he excelled.

So much for pitching horseshoes. But surely he wasn't playing this ballgame on a Sunday was my gravest thought. My mother would "give it to him" if she ever knew he was breaking her Sabbath rules. And I would "get it" too if she ever knew I had gone down to Main Street and crossed it, and had not told anyone I was leaving and where I was going. We had certain restrictions, which we usually followed. But that day Michael and I broke them despite the consequences. You can gather by now my mother was the disciplinarian in our family. She made up the rules, we followed without question.

Arriving at the farmer's field, I was amazed to see the throng and the sight unsettled me. I didn't know why, perhaps it was because there were only men I could see milling about, maybe it was the excitement in the air and because my brother caused all this excitement I may have felt he might be in harm's way, or was it because I knew he was breaking my mother's Sabbath rules, and now I was part of it. But whatever, my fears didn't hinder me. I was determined to find out what was going on.

I joined the throng of men and boys in the field. I had to burrow through to stand in front of the tall adults so I could see what was happening. I expected to find our Michael throwing the ball back and forth as he did with my brother John. Instead, I took in a very strange scene. There was someone standing with his back to me in the center of a cleared field, at ease, ball in one hand, glove in the other, gazing up at a flight of birds. Other boys threw a ball around what I later learned was called a diamond. I didn't see Michael until the "someone" turned and I realized, it was my brother standing in the middle of the field gazing at the birds. He didn't have on the Sunday suit he was wearing when he left the house soon after noon. He wore a uniform and cap like all the others on the field. I hardly recognized him. He looked so different.

The unsettled feeling overcame me again. But young as I was, I suddenly knew why. From information I had gathered along the way, I was not seeing "our" Michael, I was looking at the baseball player I had first learned about on the way down the street, who now stood where he seemed to belong. And I recall feeling a sense of loss realizing he wasn't just "our" Michael anymore. I somehow knew he also belonged to the growing crowd of strangers surrounding me who knew and claimed him. The ballplayer he now was, and they all "came to see the kid pitch" and an overwhelming feeling overcame me, an urge to reclaim him, to shout, "He's our Michael! Not yours!"

But possessive feelings were just as suddenly put aside as too much new was happening, and I was taken in and being consumed by it all. The boys in uniform were throwing baseballs, one to another, too fast for me to follow and make sense of this game. I didn't know what I was watching. Furthermore, I didn't see my brother John out there, but I knew, since he wasn't on the field, he must have been in the throng as he and Michael had left the house together.

Now I knew why they had hurried away after Sunday dinner. I wondered why he wasn't on the field throwing the ball to Michael, and why Michael wasn't throwing the ball and playing the game with the other boys instead of looking up in the sky and kicking the dirt.

In the meantime, around what I knew as home plate, first and third base, the crowd was three and four deep with men and boys pressed together from home plate to third and home to first. There were very few women with the men, and no young girls I could see. But then, I wasn't interested in looking about and being seen by someone who could tell my mother. I stood in front of everyone on the third base side, a few feet away from what I had heard called the "bag." All around me was talk of my brother and the men and teen boys making bets, passing a "pint" around, and lighting up. I began to worry the cigar and cigarette smoke would get into my Sunday clothes like it did my father's, who smoked cigars, and what was I going to say to my mother when I arrived home?

But all this excitement about my brother pitching that filled the air overtook me too. All fears and worries were replaced by interest in the surrounding activity. Trying to figure out this game, I wondered when my brother would start.

Suddenly, I heard a shout, "PLAY BALL!" and the din that followed pierced my young ears. There was a young lad in uniform now standing near the "bag" so close if I reached out I could touch him. But my eyes were trained on what I now accepted was a baseball player. My brother, the baseball pitcher, stood alone in the middle of the field, everyone looking at him and screaming. Then he moved. Suddenly, there was complete silence. He threw the ball and all hell broke loose. He threw a STRIKE! That's what everyone came to see and they all were overjoyed.

After that, every time my brother threw the ball, the crowd roared. It was not long before I was caught up in the excitement, no longer any scared feelings, and I soon learned he was throwing strikes.... and you cheered, and when the umpire called a ball....you hollered "YOU NEED GLASSES!" or you groaned, or yelled to my brother, "GET IT IN THERE, BOY!" I found myself joining in following the enthusiastic crowd as if I knew what was happening, yelling to my brother, "MICKEEEEE! THROW A STRIKE!" At the end of the game when his side won, or it seemed from those around me, Michael won, when I raced across the field to reclaim him and tell him I was there, and saw him throw strikes, and win, I couldn't reach him because of the players and men surrounding him – hugging him and pummeling him on the back. Since I was small and was squeezed in the midst of all these cigar smoking, drinking, betting, overjoyed men, I saw the "pass" into my brother's pants – down into his waistband and smarty pants I was, I knew it was bet money, for I had heard some of the men around me betting on the number of strikes he would throw, and so discovered the men who had bet on him and the game shared what they won.

I learned a great deal about my brother and baseball that day. And being the little sister, a girl, I never had the opportunity to bask in his fame since I was now part of his secret life, along with my brother John. I was growing up fast, for I also learned John won a great deal of money placing bets on the game and Michael. No wonder John wasn't playing. They were gambling! That was something to remember too for future use.

Later, getting Michael alone, I told him what I saw the men do. That was when he threatened to "let me have one" if I opened my mouth and told on him. And since he threatened me, I played my "ace in the hole" I had been saving up for the right moment to spring it. I told him I knew about stealing too and confessed I overheard him and John talking one night about stealing bases. I knew I had him with that one because that's when he really lost it, calling me, among other things, "a crazy kid" and saying he'd give me "a fat lip" if I told anyone lies about him and John stealing, and further, he'd tell on me for crossing Main Street and being at the Sunday baseball game in the farmer's field.

These were just idle threats because we both knew one of our rules was boys did not hit girls. We also knew rules could be broken, as just had been that Sunday by both of us. I came home with both brothers, so didn't have to explain my absence from home.

But that day was also when I got a lesson in the art of the "deal." What did a ten-year-old kid know about wheeling and dealing with two older brothers? But I was soon to learn. I wouldn't tell if he and John took me to the Saturday matinees at the movie theater. It was the first thing I could think of in the heat of the moment. I had to strike while the iron was hot. Some may call it blackmail, but we called it wheeling and dealing, as in "I'll make you a deal" or "Let's make a deal." I soon learned it was really a bad deal, for I didn't take into account my brothers thought of us girls as "pests" to be tolerated. But a deal was a deal and I couldn't wait until Saturday. I was thrilled to know I was finally going to the movies with them – even if my brothers didn't like it.

My brothers hated the fact they had to take their little sister with them to the movies, or anywhere else. None of their friends had a kid sister tag along, and as soon as we were out of sight of our house, they made me walk behind them as if they didn't know me. They had longer legs and walked faster, and sometimes they'd run, then walk, and tired me out in my determination to keep up with them.

They told me the movie theater was called "The Rat Hole" and when we went into the movie theater they told me why. They warned there were rats running around the floor in the dark, looking to take a bite out of dangling feet. Then they left me sitting alone with my legs curled under me, frightened in the dark theater while the cowboys and Indians whooped it up and killed each other, and in the serial that followed, the train barreled down the track and a terrified girl had been bound by the villains and left on the railroad track to die. On the way home when I tearfully told them I had been scared they again threatened me with worse if I "told on them." They knew how to get rid of me fast – scare me. I was deathly afraid of the dark, and they knew it. And rats chewing off my toes! Ugh!

But a bargain was a bargain. I didn't tell on them. So, they got away with it for even as a child I kept my word – but never made a bad deal with them again. I had learned my lesson in dealing. Nevertheless, without me squealing, my brother's fame in the sport of baseball soon found its way to my father, and it wasn't long before my mother found out too about Michael playing baseball on the Sabbath.

And he was grounded.

But by that time he had won enough fame and games to satisfy himself, and he was not too unhappy about it because he had a stash of bills under the corner of the rug in the bedroom he shared with John, which I discovered when the rug flipped up as my younger sister, Mildred, and I were snooping around their room. Without getting caught, I might add.

He didn't seem to have a care knowing baseball season was over for him because big league baseball season was in full swing and he still had his glove and ball, and enough admiring friends who came around with a glove, ready to "catch" him.

When he was sixteen Michael quit school, and soon afterwards he left home. Later, I heard he was "down in the minors" but I wasn't interested enough in baseball at the time to even ask about it. It went in one ear and out the other. Then I heard he was working in Massachusetts. I didn't know why he didn't stay with the team. Evidently, what he was doing in regard to baseball was no big deal in our family, so I don't recall any conversation about baseball and Michael as a teen.

But years later, when talking baseball with him, I recalled Michael was "down in the minors" and asked him about it.

His face broke into a huge grin and, chuckling, he tossed off, "You know me, women and booze." He laughed heartily in remembrance of all the women in his life as a kid.

So I laughed too.

Evidently, his choices in life held no regrets in regard to baseball. But I wish now I had probed further or had asked John what transpired because Michael would have confided in him, and he would have known what happen to a promising baseball career as a result of the "women and booze" while in the minors.

I claimed his glove and a baseball later, and I subsequently gave his glove and the baseball signed by players on his team in the minors to his great nephew, Christopher, when he was in the little leagues. In high school, he made us proud of his prowess on second base. Christopher was caught by a photographer flying up in the air making an out on second base, and the photo landed on the front page of the Sports Section of our local Newport Beach newspaper – not once but twice. It wasn't "women and booze" that claimed Christopher, but architecture.

Each year I knew 'twas spring when I heard the sound like no other – the first "crack of the bat" – and I'd run out the front door of our house across from the park baseball diamond and there were the Little Leaguers, five and six-year-olds, suited up. I watched them, when they got that bat in their hands, their attitude and stance changed turning little boys into baseball players worthy of any league. They changed right before my eyes, as did Michael from my brother to a baseball player that day in the farmer's field many, many years ago when I saw him pitch strikes and win my very first baseball game.

As I write, it's now spring and once again I hear, "PLAY BALL!" So, I sit in my wicker chair on the low brick-walled terrace across from the park baseball diamond and watch. And even if they swing and miss, or they can't outrun the caught and thrown ball, the Little Leaguers still have that "something" that brands them baseball players. And when they get a hit and run the bases, cap flying off, that "something" shouts, "I'm Mantle!" "I'm Griffey!"

So, through the years when spring bursts forth, I always remember other springs and the shout "PLAY BALL," and how I listened for the sound like no other – the "crack of the bat."

Around Our Dinner Table

V.K., our cousin, took violin lessons for years. Well, that's not true. Her father paid for violin lessons, for years.

As she grew older, the only way she could leave the house evenings to meet and hang out with her girlfriends was to tell her parents she was in the school band and was going to rehearsals. So, she forever carried that violin case to phantom rehearsals all through high school, as well as to phantom violin lessons.

After graduation, everywhere V.K. went, the violin, which everyone now referred to as "V.K.'s Fiddle," still went too. Even when she was no longer living at home, each time you saw the fiddle case, you knew V.K. was around somewhere.

She never left home without that fiddle, yet few had heard her play.

V.K. was full of laughs. She always knew the latest jokes, and was abreast of the latest gossip – along with having her ear to the ground for grand openings, political rallies, auctions, sales, and all the freebee's. She was fun to have around; a great gal.

The Fiddler

We were all living at Journal Square in Jersey City, my sister Micki, my brother John, and I shared an apartment, and cousin V.K. had one down the street nearby, so we saw each other almost daily.

Late one evening, V.K. came by – with her violin case. But this night was different. She wanted Micki and me to go with her to the Treat Hotel in Newark to a jam session after midnight. Micki withdrew to get dressed. I immediately bowed out. V.K tried to wheedle me to accompany them, but I didn't want to stay up all night having my eardrums battered.

"Who's going to be there?" I asked. Maybe it would be someone I'd like to hear play and meet.

"I have no idea, I just heard about it and thought I'd go and sit in," V.K. said.

"You mean you're going to crash it? And play?"

"I'm bringing my violin, they won't throw us out."

Micki came back into the living room all ready to go, looking stunning, as she always did.

"Did you know you're going to crash this jam session?" I thought I'd warn her. "Be prepared to be thrown out on your ear."

"Don't pay any attention to her, Mick. Let's go." V.K. picked up her violin case and hustled Micki out before I could change her mind.

I heard Micki return at daybreak. I was anxious to learn if V.K. played with the "boys" since it was obvious they weren't given the boot. But I had to wait. Micki slept throughout the day and we didn't see her until dinnertime.

Around the dinner table with the gang, Micki said they went to the Treat Hotel and V.K.'s violin case was their entrée.

"It was all rather easy. V.K. had her violin case, and we just walked to the desk and asked where the jam session was being held, and they told us."

"That fiddle certainly comes in handy," I laughed.

"They gave us the room number and floor, and directed us to the elevator," Micki continued, ignoring me. "I began to get butterflies in my stomach, you know me. I thought this was too easy. So, I began to get worried."

Micki went on to say it was all in vain because they arrived on the floor, and went to an open door, looked in – they saw musicians with their instruments, and as they entered, each called out their names. It was very laid back and congenial. The musicians who were there came from clubs around Jersey and Lower Manhattan where they were playing. Everyone was very friendly, so she and V.K. pulled up a chair, and sat down. A few more musicians arrived after them, and soon the music started. Matt Dennis, the singer, who was playing at the Blue Mirror night club was the last to arrive.

I was surprised no one questioned them. They were the only females – young ladies who looked too young to be out after midnight. "When they were all ready to go, what did V.K. do?" I asked.

"She had her violin out, so she sat right in with them."

"And she played?" We all queried in amazement.

"Well, I saw her pushing that bow back and forth," Micki said. "I don't know if she was playing or sawing. The music was wild. The place was jumping!"

There was a reason we were so curious about V.K. jamming with all these musicians who were playing with the big bands. The only time anyone heard V.K. play the fiddle was when we were all out on the town, most of the time in the Village in Lower Manhattan, closing up some bar, then a not-too-sober friend would shout, "V.K., play us a tune!"

And obligingly, V.K. would open the case, take out the bow and fiddle, and play.

We'd all stand up at attention and loudly sing along. "My country tis of thee, sweet land of liberty…" to the very end.

The truth.

V.K. only played one song we all called, "My country tis of thee." As in: "Here comes, or where is, my country tis of thee?" referring to V.K.

She played with a fiddle kept in tune. We were loud and sounded like we all could take singing lessons – but we ended the evening and closed many a bar with everyone in the joint singing along, while with the great dignity the song deserved, V.K. fiddled, "My country tis of thee…" And looked like a diva playing Carnegie Hall doing so.

Maybe jamming after hours in the private suite at the Treat Hotel in Newark, New Jersey with the Boys from the Big Bands, in the wee small hours, V.K. jazzed up "My country tis of thee....sweet land of liberty... "

She never let us know.

• • •

NATIONAL ANTHEM

After recalling the night V.K. and Micki went to the Treat Hotel and crashed a jam session with the Boys from the Big Bands, and since we were laughing and talking about the times we closed up bars with "My Country Tis of Thee," it only followed that the natural progression was, you guessed it, our National Anthem – "The Star Spangled Banner." Of course, that would lead to how difficult it was to sing, which leads to each of us attempting to sing it. We all should have been arrested. That is one difficult song for those of us who can't carry a tune to wrap our vocal cords around. Even when I hear professional singers, I mentally help them through the high notes, and seem to let out my breath when ended. It makes one wonder how many are clapping because the singer made it through or because of patriotism.

After doing "The Star Spangle Banner" an injustice vocally, it naturally leads to what the National Anthem should be changed to – which leads to a sing-a-long. So, we had "God Bless America," that Kate Smith long, long ago sang beautifully, and people thought it was, or should replace, "The Star Spangled Banner." Then we had "America" – better known as "My Country, Tis of Thee" –we all decided was much easier to sing than "The Star Spangled Banner." After that came "America, the Beautiful," or as everyone calls it, "Oh, Beautiful for Spacious Skies" that got a chorus of full voices raising the roof. This one everyone seemed to agree really expresses America.

But when it came to the discussion about changing the National Anthem from "The Star Spangled Banner" – there was too much history, flag and country sentiment, "...the rockets' red glare, the bombs bursting in air," and "... land of the free and home of the brave," for anyone of us to want to change it.

Everyone agreed they would miss the loss of the symbolism of the large waving ground covering flag, the fireworks, and the fly-overs opening all our sporting events.

Oh yes, we ended the evening with "My country tis of thee, sweet land of liberty...let freedom ring!"

Wouldn't you know when the last note was sung, a wise guy said, "Someone should have brought a fiddle."

I thought we did pretty well without it. But what do I know? I can't carry a tune.

Wishes

Meggie awoke with a leg thrown across her belly. She looked over at her five-year-old who had once again crept into her bed during the night. She turned, then kissed the top of his curly head as she reached out and tickled him awake. After wrestling for a few minutes of giggling, she rolled out of bed.

Jamie, now wide awake, trailed her to the bathroom where Meggie watched as he splashed some water on his face, and brushed his teeth.

"I don't know why I have to brush teeth when I'm going to eat and they'll get dirty," he complained.

"Well, if you get them dirty, you can brush again."

"I don't want to brush, but I have to eat," he groaned. "I'm hungry now."

"Put on your shorts and t-shirt, go and get some orange juice and cereal. I have to call about my car, then I'll join you," she said running her hand lovingly through his uncombed curls as she left for her office at the end of the hall, calling back to him, "Save some juice for me!"

Distressed, Meggie dropped her phone on the desk. Her car that was in the garage for repairs would not be ready until late afternoon tomorrow. She had started toward the door to join Jamie for breakfast when he came running in to her office shouting:

"Mommy! Mommy! Come. Quick!"

"Jamie! No running in the house," she reminded him.

"But, Mommy, come quick! You got your wish!"

"Calm down. What wish?"

"The wish you made! The one for a new car when our car stopped in the middle of traffic yesterday, and it had to be towed away!" He jumped around with excitement. "You got your wish, come see!"

Jamie grabbed her hand and pulled her along the hall, out to the rear terrace. Teetering on the edge of the pool, sparkling in the morning sun, was a new silver sport car.

Meggie blinked to make sure she wasn't seeing things, then momentarily closed her eyes. But when she opened them, the car hadn't disappeared. She turned her head and to the far right was the hole in the six foot high hedge through which the car had entered, evidently losing it on the curve.

Jamie danced around with excitement. He couldn't stand still. "Just what you wished for!" he kept shouting.

"Settle down. Settle down," Meggie said trying to calm him. "It isn't exactly what I had in mind when I wished for a new car." She was more surprised than excited.

"But your wish came true!" Jamie insisted.

Meggie stood, gazing at the automobile. She should check it, but she was afraid to leave the terrace, fearing the car teetering over the pool would move and tip in. She noted the driver's side door was open. So, whoever lost control of the car walked away uninjured.

Meggie wondered what time it happened. She didn't hear any noises during the night.

"What are we going to do, Mommy?"

"I don't think that's our problem."

If there was a note or I.D. in the glove compartment, it would stay there. She was not going near. And admonished Jamie, "Don't leave this terrace," as she went into the house and returned to take a few photos.

No one called or came by for the automobile. Of course, they wouldn't phone; they didn't have her telephone number. But, surely, whoever it was, they were coming for their car. She was aware it was too costly to abandon.

Jamie differed.

He was certain this was the answer to her wish, and it would be useless trying to convince him otherwise until the car was claimed by its owner, so Meggie didn't try.

"We'll go about our day until someone comes by for the car," she said. "You can read your new book, and then build something with your Legos."

Meggie didn't call any of her friends. She didn't want them beating down her door for a "look see." She had too much work to do. She worked at home, and she was behind in her scheduled calls and overnight emails. Meggie finally calmed Jamie enough to settle him down reading the new book he had wanted so badly – then to work herself.

"Mommy," she heard a little voice say, "my tummy is telling me it wants something to eat."

Meggie checked the time.

It was past his lunchtime. She was surprised he hadn't interrupted her before this. "I know what we can do to satisfy that," she said hurrying him down the hallway to the kitchen.

"How?" he questioned.

"Well, how about your favorite?"

"Yes! Yes!" he cried, as he ran to get placemats and take them outside to the terrace table, shouting, "Your car's still there!"

Ignoring him, Meggie continued fixing him his favorite peanut butter and jelly sandwich, and readied cantaloupe as a treat with vanilla ice cream for desert. Since the child in her demanded, she had the same. They ate lunch on the terrace overlooking the garden, pool, and shining silver sport car.

Lately, Jamie had been pestering for a kitty, but a growing active child of five was enough for Meggie without having a pet underfoot at this time in their lives.

Now since Jamie felt her wish for a car had come true, he tested, "Maybe if I wish for a kitty, I'll get my wish too."

"I wouldn't waste a wish for a kitty if I were you. I don't think it will come true and you'll be disappointed."

"But you weren't disappointed. Your wish came true and the car is bigger than a kitty," he reasoned.

"The car isn't mine; it'll be gone before the day is over."

It bewildered Meggie someone hadn't already been by to claim the auto, but she didn't let Jamie know she had any concerns.

Meggie rose from the table. "Come on, time I got back to work, and you, to your nap."

They put the paper plates in the trash and carried the placemats and silver indoors to the kitchen, then proceeded to Jamie's room. He kicked off his sneakers and jumped onto the bed. Meggie put a throw over him that he shrugged away and reached for his cuddling pillow.

"I'll wake you if someone comes with a tow truck to take the car away. I know you want to see the tow truck," Meggie promised and went off to work.

Therefore, before Jamie dozed off, she didn't hear him whisper into his pillow, "I wish I had a kitty! I really do! I wish I had a kitty!"

They watched and waited, but no one came by for the car. It became mystifying, and now worrisome. She thought it may be a stolen car. Meggie knew she should call the police, and vowed to make the call if no one turned up today. She felt she had waited too long before doing so.

By late afternoon, rain clouds had formed, the skies darkened, and while eating dinner, the rainstorm hit hard. The sound of the rain beating down on the terrace joined by another sound caused Jamie to stop feeding his face to listen.

"Do you hear that, Mommy?" Jamie inquired, his voice rising.

Meggie listened. "I don't hear anything but the storm."

"I hear it!"

Jamie's excitement caused her to stop eating and listen again.

The soulful mewing of a cat was heard over the pelting rain. Pushing away from the table, Jamie ran to the sliding glass door.

"Don't open the door!" Meggie shouted as she followed him.

Hands on the door pull, Jamie halted, "But it's a kitty out in the rain; it's crying!"

Nudging Jamie aside, Meggie flipped on the terrace light, looked out at a drenched, scrawny kitten, begging to be let in out of the rain, and slowly opened the door.

Jamie immediately reached around her, and scooped up the animal hugging it to his chest, crying, "I got my wish! I got my wish! Just like you, Mommy! I got my wish!"

Meggie looked out the window from the sad sight in Jamie's arms to another sad sight still teetering on the edge of the pool being battered by the storm.

Dinner forgotten, the next hour was spent bathing the kitten and bathing Jamie while warning him not to get attached to the kitten. "It probably belongs to someone and became frightened and lost in the storm."

But, all that concerned Jamie was he had wished really hard for a kitty and his wish was granted.

All Meggie could think about was she now had to find the owner of the kitten, along with the owner of the car still in her back garden.

In the morning, the breakfast conversation was all about the storm and what it left at their doorstep passing through. The now clean kitten looked as if it had been abandoned and neglected, but Meggie knew she would have to put "Found" posters around the neighborhood in spite of Jamie believing his wish for a kitten was granted.

Meggie spent the next hour trying to convince a five-year-old it was not true that all you had to do was wish for something and it would turn up in your backyard. Also, she needed to make him understand the kitty had to be taken to a vet before he could cuddle with it, while Jamie's primary concern was the door was not to be opened or the kitty would be lost again.

While Jamie cut more newspaper for the small cardboard box with newspaper that had been assembled to serve as a litter box the prior night, Meggie, again, reminded him the kitty may not be staying.

They fed the kitty tuna and Jamie requested when it was time to feed the kitty lunch, he'd have tuna for his lunch too.

"That's fine," Meggie agreed. "We'll all have tuna, only we'll have a salad."

After seeing Jamie sitting on the floor in the den with his books, games, puzzles – and a contented kitten asleep nearby on one of his t-shirts, Meggie reminded Jamie someone may be coming for the automobile today as she left for her office.

The kitty, who turned out to be a little beauty after washing off all the guck that came with it, had settled in and made itself right at home. Jamie wasn't reading his book, he was watching the kitten sleeping, snuggled in his t-shirt. "I know I got my wish, like Mommy did," he murmured, talking to himself. "Now, I only have one more thing to wish for," and he scrunched his eyes closed, wishing really hard he said, "I wish I had a daddy!" then sighing, opened his eyes and picked up his book.

It wasn't much later, busy at work in her office, when Meggie was interrupted by the chiming of the doorbell.

"Doorbell!" shouted an excited Jamie, who came running out of the den.

"I hear it!" Meggie yelled back.

It chimed again as she joined Jamie anxiously waiting at the door. Meggie opened it.

There stood a jean clad six foot, rugged, hunk of a man. Even with a less than perfect nose that looked as if it had been shaped by a fist, he was head turning.

At the sight of Meggie, a slow smile broke out on his face and, holding her gaze, jangling his key ring, he chuckled, "I think you have my car in your back garden, teetering on your pool."

Meggie realized she was staring at him, returned his smile, but before she could speak, Jamie who had peeked around Meggie and saw God's gift to women gazing at his mom and grinning, liked what he saw, and pumped his fist high in the air with a happy, thunderous yell,

"YES!"

Around Our Dinner Table

When I began writing, as I've said, I wanted to write a book of short short stories of one sentence. I am aware there are one sentence novels, but it was not my intention to make readers go mad reading one, as it would me in even attempting to write one. But when I started writing the short short stories of one sentence, in that I failed. The stories took over and wrote at will. So, some are short and some are long....and not one sentence. Then when I finished writing my last story, to my surprise "Footsteps" popped up and wrote itself, as fast as I could type it.

Footsteps

Throughout time, footsteps where you walked…as in sand, a wind, or tide will erase, and those footsteps are seen no more….and as you walk through life, present becomes past, and all your footsteps, though not seen, have become a memory…even those footsteps in sand having been erased by wind or tide.

ALICE MARCHAK was born in Taylor (a suburb of Scranton), Pa., moved at an early age to Hollywood, California. She worked at Paramount Studio as Secretary to Director John Farrow for several years, and two years for Producer Irving Asher, then two years as Secretary to George Englund and Marlon Brando, Sr., Producers for Marlon Brando's film company Pennebaker before becoming Personal Assistant to Marlon. She left Paramount to work for Marlon in his home, and at her home office in Newport Beach where she still resides.

Alice has co-authored *Supersecs* with Linda Hunter, and has written the definitive books about the actor and her years as Personal Assistant and friend to Marlon, and guardian to his son, Christian, in her two books *Me and Marlon* and More *Me and Marlon*.

She also wrote *Christmas: A Child is Born*, and *Easter: Hosanna in the Highest*.